I0718444

Cobble: Elves and the Shoemaker Retold

DEMELZA CARLTON

A tale in the Romance a Medieval Fairy Tale series

Lost Plot Press

ISBN: 978-1-925799-31-6

DEDICATION

In memory of Oma.
Because 103 is more than most will ever see.

One

This pair, Alba vowed, would be perfect. She used a cloth to wet the leather, just a little, not too much. Then she pressed the stamp against the smooth hide. A few gentle taps with her hammer and it was done. Now all she needed to do was paint the embossed flower so that the jewel-like colours would catch the eye of some passing lady, and yet another one of her creations would grace the King's court. They were no match for the christening shoes she'd made for the Crown Princess, but she'd sent them up to the palace. Once the King saw them, surely he'd declare her the Royal Shoemaker, as her father had been.

Alba sat back and sighed. If only her father could have seen them. He would be proud. But he'd passed the previous winter, leaving her in her brothers' care. As though they cared.

Speak of the devil, and he shall appear.

Her brothers' laughing voices sounded from the street.

Alba hurried to hide her embossing tools, and the half-made shoe. If her brothers found the cunningly crafted flowers and other shapes, they would sell them for sure and drink the proceeds. Never mind that she needed them to make a living. She could not be the Royal Shoemaker if she could no longer make shoes.

The bag tucked neatly into its rafter hiding spot, and the thatch smoothed into place as if it had never been disturbed. A good thing, too, for her brothers' good humour died the moment they entered the house.

"We need to go," Gad said, grabbing her arm.

"Where are we going? Should I pack?" Alba asked.

"No time," Onni said, peering through the window. "Jordanes has summoned the guards to evict us and they are already on their way."

Alba tore out of her brother's grasp. "Why would our landlord evict us? The shoes I make earn more than enough to pay the rent. Only last week he stopped by to commission a pair as a gift to his wife for Christmas. He never mentioned you'd forgotten to pay the rent. Father left us plenty of money…"

"Father's money is gone. We haven't paid rent since he died. And we need to go now or we'll be taken to the cells beneath the castle where we'll die as debtors." Gad seized her arm again and dragged her from her seat. "Now, Alba. We promised Father we would take care of you. Do you know what happens to women in the castle dungeons?"

Alba had heard all sorts of horrible stories about the dungeons, but she'd never imagined she might feature in one. "No," she began.

"Then you don't want to find out. Come, or all is lost!"

"But my things…" she faltered.

Onni took her other arm and between them, her brothers dragged her to the back door. "No time," Onni said. "We can buy more when we are free of Jordanes and his guards. Do you want to live free or die in prison?"

"I want to live," Alba said, risking a glance back over her shoulder at the cottage where she had spent all of her life. Without her tools, would she ever make shoes again?

"Then you must run!"

Bracketed by her brothers, Alba took to her heels, leaving behind everything else she had ever known or loved.

Two

"Brogan, I believe?" the well-dressed man asked. "I'm Jordanes."

Brogan forced himself to smile, an expression that felt wrong on his face so soon after his father's death. "I'm Brogan the shoemaker. I heard you had a suitable shop for rent?"

Jordanes' smile seemed genuine. "That I do. That I do. Quite a bargain, too. Shall we?" He gestured for Brogan to follow him, and set off up the hill toward the castle.

Plodding along behind his prospective new

landlord, Brogan let out a breath he hadn't known he'd been holding. Brogan's older brother, Gereon, had inherited their father's shop. Father had left some money to help Brogan set up his own shop, provided he was far enough away from his brother not to hurt his business.

Well, Brogan couldn't get much further away from Gereon than this, and still be within Kasmirus. Across the river and halfway up the hill on the Royal Road that led from the main gate to the castle on the hill. Gereon could make boots for half the townsfolk, but if Brogan could catch the eye of some passing nobleman or woman on their way up to the castle…why, he could prove to himself and his family that he was just as good a shoemaker as his father and his brother, if not better.

"It's been vacant for some time, so it may need some repairs. I will charge you lower rent for that, of course," Jordanes said without turning around. "You won't find a better location anywhere in Kasmirus, of that I can assure you. Before the previous tenant died, he was the most famed shoemaker in the city.

Why, he even made the King's and Queen's shoes."

The Royal Shoemaker had lived there? Brogan would be a fool to refuse. "Show me," he said eagerly.

Jordanes pushed open the door to a house that looked much like the others in the street. The red bricks showed a little more through the lime whitewash, true, but it was nothing a day's labour wouldn't fix. Brogan could wield a brush as well as the next man.

"What are you doing here?" Jordanes demanded.

Brogan entered the cottage just in time to see two small boys scamper out the back door.

"Looking for ghosts. Everyone knows this place is haunted!" one boy called back over his shoulder.

Jordanes laughed, pulling out a handkerchief to wipe his forehead. It was a long moment before he met Brogan's eyes. "Silly boys. Children have such wild imaginations," Jordanes said.

Haunted. So that was why the rent was so low. Brogan looked up, expecting to see some signs of disrepair, but the worst he saw was dust and cobwebs. Things that could be cleaned.

"There's a large cellar beneath the house, and even a sleeping loft," Jordanes continued, pointing.

The ladder to the loft didn't look too sturdy, but nor had the one he and Gereon had scrambled up to their own beds every night Brogan could remember.

"Are the previous tenant's tools still here?" Brogan asked. He had some of his own, but Gereon had kept most of his father's things.

Jordanes shrugged. "Perhaps in the cellar."

Brogan nodded. Perhaps was worth a hope. Once he'd made the sleeping loft and the main workroom liveable, then he could tackle the cellar. Why, he could be making shoes for the King by next week.

"I'll take it," Brogan decided.

Jordanes grinned. "A wise decision. I'm sure you won't regret it."

Looking around, Brogan was certain the man was right. No, not just any man. His new landlord. Brogan smiled broadly. "I'll move in tomorrow."

Three

Brogan had thought he'd need a handcart, but he was disappointed to discover that all of his possessions fitted into a sack. A heavy sack, that took some effort to heft onto his shoulder, but a single sack, nonetheless.

Gereon's wife, Tihana, a quietly capable mouse of a woman, handed him a second small sack of food to take with him. She wouldn't miss him, Brogan knew — one less man to cook and clean for meant half the work. Perhaps now she and Gereon would have the children Gereon longed for.

And Brogan would be able to sleep without trying to ignore their muffled fumbling in the dark as the pair engaged in marital relations a few feet away from him.

Maybe he'd have a wife of his own one day – when he had an established shoemaking business, and something to offer a girl. Right now, all he owned sat in a sack that bounced uncomfortably against his back as he crossed the bridge and headed up the hill to his new home.

The workroom was dim in the morning light, for the sun had not risen high enough to reach the windows yet. Brogan dropped his burden on the work table, sending up a puff of dust. The place had been deserted for some time, it seemed, judging by the thickness of the dust layer smothering everything. He would soon bring life back to the building, he swore.

Something on the tabletop caught his eye. Wiping away the dust to see it better, he found four letters carved into the wooden surface. These weren't the work of a bored boy like he'd once been, cutting out leather for his father when he wanted to play outside. No, this was the work of an artist, who wished their name remembered.

ALBA, he read, running his fingertips over the intricate curls of the letters as they sprouted into a flowering vine that flourished in a ring around the word. Wasn't that the name of a country far to the west, on the edge of the world? A country someone had loved enough to carve this into the table so they might forever remember it. He hoped whoever they were, they'd made it home.

He rested his hand on the table so he could reach for the bag of food from Tihana. An ominous crack sounded from under the table and Brogan jumped back. Just in time, too — the legs gave way and the edge of the solid tabletop crashed to the floor where his feet had been. If he hadn't moved, his toes would have been crushed.

Brogan let out a breath he hadn't realised he was holding, but he was too hasty. The boards beneath him creaked, then squealed, as a hole appeared in the floor that swallowed the table whole and belched up a cloud of choking dust.

Coughing, Brogan peered down into the

cellar, where his table and his belongings now dwelled. Edging around the wall, avoiding the gaping hole he didn't want to fall into, he made his way to the cellar stairs, hoping they wouldn't break beneath him.

Perhaps the place would need more work than he thought to turn it into a shop suitable for kings. No matter. He would see it through. Dreams were all good and well, but he knew it took hard work to succeed in the world, and Brogan would do all within his power to see his dreams came to fruition.

But first, he had to go downstairs to retrieve his dinner.

Alba hid in the shadows beneath the stairs, watching the stranger. It had been a long time since she'd last heard whistling in the house, and yet that's the sound he made. The man's table had fallen through the floor, but he still managed to whistle a cheerful tune as he retrieved his things. What manner of man whistled while his house fell down around him? A mad one, that was certain.

He strode up the stairs with a confident step, and only then did she see his shoes. Finely made boots over his wool hose, though both were plain. That made him a merchant or artisan of some kind, able to afford finery but without the need to wear it anywhere but his feet. A man who appreciated a pair of fine boots might not be as mad as she'd first thought.

With every bit of her being, she wanted to stretch her hand out and touch the leather, to see if it was as soft as it appeared. A man who cared for his boots was a rarity indeed.

Reluctantly, she restrained herself. What good would it do to reveal herself? She could not touch some stranger's boots. She hadn't touched a shoe in…so long. Longer than she knew, hidden here in the dark all alone.

Well, alone but for her brothers.

And if her brothers had their way, she would never touch a shoe again. She sighed, slumping to sit on the dirt cellar floor.

Hours later, her brothers found her under the stairs.

"What was all the noise, then?" Gad asked.

Alba gestured at the fallen pile of timber. "The table fell apart, and the floor collapsed beneath it."

Onni's teeth gleamed in the dark as he grinned. "Did it really? The ghost must have unfastened the legs somehow."

Ghosts didn't take apart tables. But Onni did. Alba glared at him.

He continued on without a care, "I wish I'd been here to see it. When the house falls down around our ears, then we'll be released from the curse. And we'll be free!"

Alba wasn't sure curses worked that way. "What if we're trapped here, house or no house?"

Gad waved away her worries. "We won't be. There's always a way out. Always. Don't you remember the stories Mother used to tell us? It's all about being clever and outwitting the witch!"

Alba racked her brain, but she could think of no story where thieves had won against a witch. Perhaps they had heard different tales to those her mother had told her, of knights and princesses and love.

"This man will not be so easy to frighten," she warned them.

Onni laughed. "What are you talking about?

Of course he will be! The house is haunted as haunted can be. I heard some of the local children tell him about the ghosts here. He'll have packed up and left before the church bells ring for Sunday mass."

Alba bit her lip and didn't reply. Her brothers might be right – they usually were – but this time, she hoped the man might stay. She smelled change in the air, and with it came hope.

But hope for what, she couldn't say.

Perhaps he should have apprenticed as a carpenter instead of a shoemaker, Brogan mused as he fastened his much lightened purse. Yet the new floor looked good, and was as solid as the rock the castle above was built upon. A solid foundation on which to build his business.

Wido the carpenter had even fixed his table for free, or so he said. The legs had somehow come unfastened, for the wood was as solid as ever, even after the table's trip to the cellar. Wido suggested some of the local lads might have done it as a prank, not knowing how fragile the floor beneath it was, and Brogan was inclined to agree. He and Gereon might have done the same thing ten years ago, though their father would have thrashed them for it.

Not wanting to cause trouble for the boys or their families, he kept quiet about it. If the boys returned, he wanted to ask more about the previous tenants, and why they thought the place was haunted. Brogan hadn't seen hide nor hair of a ghost since he arrived, though on reflection, ghosts had neither hide nor hair, so he wouldn't, would he?

Brogan laughed quietly to himself as he swept the floor. The workroom was ready for him to start work tomorrow, and he'd laid up a supply of leather in preparation which he'd stashed in the cellar, out of Wido's way while he worked.

He'd even found time to whitewash the walls outside. Now his shop gleamed whiter than its fellows, like fresh-fallen snow. Not that there was any snow on the street to compare it to, of course. Much too early in the year. Snow rarely set in before Christmas, and that was weeks away yet.

Brogan considered cutting out the leather tonight in the remaining light, but he decided he'd earned an afternoon off. It was Sunday, after all, and supposed to be a day of rest. He'd go visit his brother and his wife, and see how well they were getting on without him.

And get a hot meal of Tihana's cooking, for he'd sorely missed it. His own cooking skills were non-existent, and he could not yet afford a servant to do such things for him. Soon enough, he promised himself. He would sell shoes to courtiers and no longer would he have to sweep his own floors or choke down his own burned cooking.

<h1 style="text-align:center">Six</h1>

"What smells of cat's piss in here?" Onni asked.

Now that he mentioned it, Alba smelled it, too. One of the local alley cats had sneaked into the house and marked its new territory again, she assumed.

"I'm no cat!" Gad protested. "Flea-ridden ratcatchers, the lot of them!" He jumped on the spot a bit, and Alba realised why.

"You foul wretch!" she cried, batting at her brother. "What kind of fiend are you, relieving yourself on the floor, no less? Couldn't you walk a few extra steps to a chamber pot or even a bucket?"

"It already smelled like that before I got to it!" Gad insisted. "Leather fresh from the tanners, look!"

Breathing through her mouth so that she wouldn't smell the stench so much, Alba edged toward the wet sack. She nudged it open with her foot, and saw the rolled-up leather inside. Work supplies for the man who lived in the house, for she hadn't noticed them before.

Curiosity ate at her. Was he a saddler, or an armorer? She didn't dare hope he was a shoemaker, as her father had been. But whatever he intended to work the leather into, he must be quite the craftsman, to take a house along the Royal Road and all. The King and his courtiers only wanted to see merchandise fit for them when they rode along the road.

"Do that again, and I'll empty a bucket of wash water over your head," Alba told her brother.

"You do that and I'll give you a hiding you won't forget," Gad growled. "Don't interfere with what you don't understand. I'm only doing it to get rid of the man upstairs. If his leather is ruined, then he'll have to leave."

Alba opened her mouth to remind him that no amount of piss, his or anyone's, would destroy well-tanned leather. Why, the tanners used it to tan the hides in the first place. After a moment, she closed her mouth again. Perhaps her brothers didn't know. They hadn't been as eager to accompany their father to the tanner's to get fresh leather to work with as she had been – they hadn't cared for his trade at all. Too busy stealing from market stalls and pulling pranks on anyone who would fall for them.

"If he knew you'd pissed on his leather, maybe he'd turn you out instead," Alba said. Reluctantly, she turned away from the sack of supplies and forced herself to walk away. It took every bit of her willpower not to pull out a piece of leather and imagine what she might create with it.

"You've turned into a shrew, little sister," Onni complained. "You're lucky you never married, or your husband would have beat it out of you. Now we're cursed to endure it."

It was their own fault they were cursed, and no mistake, Alba thought but didn't say. What would be the point? They never listened to her, anyway.

But when they weren't looking, she pushed the sack out of the puddle and hoped she would get to see what the man upstairs created with it. She would give anything to work with leather again.

Seven

The bag of leather smelt unusually fresh, but Brogan supposed it was because the stuff was fresh – he'd only bought it from the tanner yesterday. Normally leather stayed in the cellar of his father's shop for weeks or even months before it was put to use. But here on the far side of the city, he had to find a new tanner and do business differently. Maybe a year from now, he'd have the money to stockpile stuff in the cellar. For now…

For now he could put his reconstructed table to use as he cut boots.

Brogan fell easily into a rhythm, chalking outlines for uppers and soles as he portioned the leather out into as many boots as possible. He'd bought better quality leather than his father used to work with, which meant paying more and being more careful to use every scrap. If he didn't, it could mean the difference between eating meat or cabbage next week. And Brogan had never been fond of cabbage.

After he finished with the chalk, Brogan started with the shears. But the light was failing, so he only managed to cut out the pieces for three pairs of boots before he was forced to retire for the night.

In the morning, every piece of leather was wiped clean, as though Brogan's chalk outlines had never been. But his chalk supplies told a different story.

Someone was playing a prank on him, and Brogan would not stand for it.

The sound of young boys' laughter outside decided him. Brogan stalked to the front door. Three boys chased each other in the street, laughing as they eluded one another. Brogan had been good at this game, and his longer legs now gave him the advantage. He seized the first boy who came close enough, and hauled him up by the collar. "Are you responsible for this?" He waved at the worktable through the open door.

"Me, sir? No, sir. I'm not brave enough to go into a haunted house, even if they say they stayed there a whole day and didn't see no ghosts!"

His friends approached, though not close enough to be grabbed like their compatriot. "No, he's a fraidy cat, sir," one boy volunteered helpfully. "Have you seen the ghosts?"

"What did they look like?" the other piped up.

Haunted. He'd forgotten.

Brogan let his captive down gently. "If I find you boys are playing pranks on my shop, you'll regret it," he said, trying to sound frightening.

Three pairs of eyes grew wide. "No, sir, we'd never do that. The ghosts would get us. That's their shop, it is."

As if on some pre-arranged signal, all three

bolted in the same moment, vanishing before Brogan could ask them anything else.

Multiple ghosts, not just one. But he hadn't heard or seen anything to be able to say his house was haunted. Except for the erased chalk marks, which were just plain puzzling. Only a fellow shoemaker would know how much work they'd undone, and those boys were too young to be learning a trade yet.

The ghost of the old shoemaker who'd lived here before, then, Brogan decided. A man who didn't want another to take over his shop.

"I won't be driven out by the ghost of a dead man," Brogan said softly, so no one outside would hear him talking to himself. "You hear me, ghost? This was your shop, but it's mine now. Someone must make shoes for the King now you're gone. Why not me?"

He grinned at his own daring, hoping he was right and one day he would make shoes for royalty, just like his predecessor.

In the meantime, he'd outfox his opponent. Instead of chalking all the outlines at once, he only did a sheet or two at a time, cutting them out before taking the chalk to a new sheet of leather. It was slower, but he managed to cut half his leather before the day ended.

On the morrow, his shears and chalk disappeared. Brogan searched the house from top to bottom, but they were nowhere to be found.

Swearing roundly about ghosts who wouldn't give up, he ventured out to buy new to replace what had been stolen. By the end of the third day, he had enough leather cut to craft a dozen pairs of the best boots, with a little leather left over that he thought might make shoes for a child.

Smiling, Brogan stretched out on his pallet in the loft for some well-earned rest.

Eight

The man's strong, confident strokes marked him as a master of his craft. He didn't rush as he chalked outlines on the leather, tracing perfect curves and faultless lines as though he'd been doing it all his life. Perhaps he had been, Alba thought uneasily, for he looked no older than her brothers, yet his skill easily surpassed theirs.

He must have apprenticed young, or just showed an early aptitude. Like Alba herself had, though she'd had to stand on a bench to see what her father tried to teach her brothers.

But this man was not her father, or her good-for-nothing brothers.

He took up a pair of shears and began to snip the shapes into proper pieces. Her hands itched to take up some scissors so that she might help him, working on one end of the leather while he worked on the other. So strong was the urge to join him that she nearly jumped down from her rafter hiding place to take a seat beside him.

But if she did that, he might take fright and leave, so she could no longer watch him at work. And if she could not create shoes with her own hands, it was the next best thing to watch someone else do what she longed for.

When he was asleep, her brothers wiped away his work of the previous day, and Alba nearly cried when she saw. It took all her willpower to resist putting it right, and retrace the erased chalk marks for him. But he would know the marks weren't his, for her touch was lighter and less sure, especially after so long.

So she watched, and coveted, and wished things could be different.

But fate was cruel and had never given Alba

what she wanted before…why would she relent now?

Nine

Brogan set the final boot on the table and sat back to regard his handiwork. He'd made the finest boots of his career, and it was a gratifying sight. A week's work looked wonderful, all spread out like this.

He took an oiled cloth and buffed the leather a little, just to see how nicely it caught the afternoon light. Tomorrow, he would put the boots in the window, setting them in such an enticing way that no one passing by could resist stopping to stare. Someone would purchase them, and word would spread.

Brogan rose. Such an occasion should be celebrated. He had some coins left, which would be enough to buy dinner from one of the nearby inns instead of attempting to make his own meal here.

Decided, Brogan grabbed his cloak from its hook and headed out, pulling the door shut behind him.

His fortunes were about to change. He knew it with the same certainty that the sun would rise on the morrow.

Ten

"By all that's holy, burn, damn you!" Gad hissed.

Alba's heart sank. Whatever Gad was doing, it sounded bad. She raced for the workroom, only to find it was worse than she'd imagined.

"Leather won't burn by itself," Onni said matter-of-factly. "You need tinder and fuel, like any fire. Here, I'll get some." He shimmied up to the loft and scrambled along the rafters until he stood above the worktable.

"Ha! It does burn!" Gad shouted, his concentration so intense that he didn't notice

Alba until she snatched the torch out of his hand.

"Why?" Alba cried. Tears fell unchecked as she saw the mischief her brothers had wrought.

Two pairs of boots were already blackened from their proximity to the torch, but the oilcloth draped over another pair had caught alight, and Alba didn't know how to extinguish them. It might already be too late.

"Try this!" Onni called. A shower of straw dropped onto the work table, smothering the boots in mouldy thatch. Onni grinned, his face like an evil moon in front of the sky Alba could now see clearly through the hole he'd dug through the roof.

The straw began to smoke. Then a tongue of flame licked up and the whole pile caught.

"You'll burn the whole house down! Find some water, quickly, or we'll burn alive!" Alba screamed, running for the water butt. She dipped a bucket in and pitched the contents at the fire. "Help me. Do you want to die?"

Bucket after bucket she threw, but it had as little effect as the thin trickle Gad, then Onni directed at the fire.

"May the saints send you to hell. Pissing on a fire to put it out. Get a bucket!" she ordered, but her brothers didn't listen.

They would burn long before hell, and she would burn with them. She'd reached the bottom of the water butt, and the fire still burned, fed by the new straw cascading from the roof.

In desperation, Alba fell to her knees and prayed.

Eleven

"Fire!"

Brogan heard the shouts as he sopped up the last of his stew with a crust of bread. He decided against a second cup of ale and headed out to help. Fire was the biggest scourge a city could have. Once it caught, it could burn half the town before it died. He could help with the bucket brigade, for he'd be protecting his own property as much as his neighbours'.

He couldn't see any smoke from the tavern door, so he headed up the hill toward his house. He'd have a better view from up there, he reasoned. It wasn't until he reached the Royal Road that he realised he could see smoke – and it was coming from his house.

He took to his heels as though the hounds of hell were behind him.

A woman screamed as he reached the door. It sounded like she was inside the house. Inside…his house? But that wasn't possible.

He seized the nearest offered bucket and kicked the door open. He coughed as he inhaled some of the billowing smoke, but he emptied his bucket on the blaze. And the next. And the next.

The buckets kept coming faster than he could throw them. Shadowy figures came and went, all doing the same as him. Putting the fire out, if they had to empty the river to do it.

After an eternity that might have only been a few minutes, the buckets stopped. The smoke hung in clouds, but he could see the sooty man beside him.

"Thank the saints, it's out," the stranger wheezed.

It was. Thank God, it was.

Brogan breathed a smoke-filled sigh of

relief, which only set him coughing.

When the coughing fit subsided, he surveyed the damage. His worktable and everything on it was a blackened mess. The floor was awash, and a gaping hole in the thatch above let out the smoke like a second chimney.

His house was a ruin, and the boots he'd made were gone.

Brogan wanted to sink to the floor in despair, but he knew he could not. Instead, he thanked the man beside him, and headed outside to thank everyone else who had helped.

Only when everyone had gone did he remember the woman's scream he'd heard.

"Mistress, do you need help?" he called, but he heard no answer. Unwilling to risk lighting another fire in his already damaged house, Brogan searched as much of the house as he could in the dark, but finally he had to give up. Whoever she was, the woman had gone, or he'd only imagined her.

He climbed up to the loft, which was miraculously intact, and his last thought before he drifted off to sleep was that he'd take a better look in the morning.

41

Twelve

"Ten gold pieces says he leaves first thing in the morning," Onni said, kicking aside a blackened blob that turned out to be more solid than he'd expected. "Ow!"

The kicked object tinkled. Alba raced to rescue it. Brushing aside the mouldy straw, too damp to burn, that still clung to it, she opened the bag. Inside was a gift from heaven itself: the half-made shoe she'd left the day her brothers forced her to flee. Beneath them was the box containing her tools, from her favourite hammer to her flowers, which seemed to look up at her expectantly.

Alba hugged the box to her chest. She'd forgotten about it, and her brothers' stupid prank had revealed its hiding place. She'd have to find a better place to stash her embossing patterns where her brothers would never find them.

"You don't have one gold piece, let alone ten," Gad remarked. A loud argument erupted between the two men, which gave Alba the opportunity to retreat to the cellar. Water dripped through the floorboards overhead, turning the cellar floor to mud, but she found a dry patch under the stairs. There she huddled with her treasure, wishing with all her might that she'd never need to see her brothers or a fire like that again.

It was a long time before she managed to sleep, and even then, the flames blazed through her dreams.

Thirteen

When morning came, Brogan searched his house from top to bottom, but there was no sign of any living thing except him. Certainly no woman. He must have imagined it, he decided.

"Hello?" a strange voice called.

Brogan headed up the cellar steps to find a man leaning through the window. "Can I help you?" Brogan asked, feeling a wry smile twist his lips. He was no help to anyone right now.

The man waved at something in the road behind him. "I heard you're in need of a new roof."

Brogan stepped out into the street. The stranger had a cart full of straw, and a couple of ladders already leaned against the wall. "How much will it cost to fix the damage?" Brogan asked, praying he had enough.

The stranger named a sum Brogan knew he'd never have.

Brogan's heart sank. He held out his purse to the man. "This is all I have left after the fire."

The man took it and squinted inside for a long moment. Finally, he closed his hand around the purse and dropped it into his pocket. "It'll do."

Brogan breathed a sigh of relief. "Thank you."

The thatcher set to work.

Brogan retreated inside what was left of his house to see what he could salvage. The table had survived, though it was scorched black in places, but the boots were burned beyond repair. If Brogan hadn't known better, he'd have thought the fire started in his new boots, but that was ridiculous. The kitchen fire was on the other side of the workroom. There was no way sparks could have reached the table, let alone the boots on it, from there.

The fire must have started in the roof, then, he decided. Though how…he'd heard no lightning or thunder, and there'd been no sign of a storm last night. Unless someone had deliberately set fire to the roof…

But why? Who could hate him so much they wanted to burn down his house? And why had they waited for him to leave before doing it? Surely they'd have wanted to burn him with it, if they truly hated him.

"It were ghosts, it were!" an excited boy's voice shouted outside. "I saw the whole thing. The roof just fell in, like an invisible hand scooped it out from the inside, and then smoke came pouring out."

Ghosts. What sort of ghosts played with fire? Brogan had never heard of such a thing.

But he had heard a woman scream. A very real woman, though she'd run off before he could find her. Whoever she was, perhaps she had been the target of the attack on his house.

If he could find her, whoever she was, then

Brogan might have some answers.

But in the meantime, he had a mess to clean up, to see if he could pick up some of his livelihood from the still-warm ashes.

At noon, one of his neighbours sent their daughter over with some food for Brogan. Brogan thanked the girl for her family's charity, for he had no other food left in the house and precious little else.

The girl blushed and ducked her head, her hands lingering on the sack just long enough to touch Brogan's fingers. She was comely enough, and of an age to marry, he realised with a sinking heart.

One day she might make a good wife to some deserving man, but today was not that day, and Brogan was not the man. He could not support himself, let alone a family. As it was, there was a very real possibility that he'd have to move back in with his brother and his wife on the morrow.

Unless he had shoes to sell. One pair that had miraculously survived the fire, or enough leather to make one last pair. The perfect pair to catch someone's eye as they passed, and came into the shop to commission more. What other hope did he have?

48

Fourteen

Some time around dawn, Alba climbed into the rafters and settled in a spot where the fire hadn't touched the roof, but she could survey the damage. Tears streaked down her cheeks as she saw what her brothers had done. If she saw them or spoke to them this morning, she would only have harsh words for them, so she was glad they kept out of her sight.

She didn't wait long before the master shoemaker, whose name she still did not know, climbed down from the loft. His shoulders slumped as he surveyed what was left of his house. For a moment, he looked like he might cry, too, but he stuck his head in the refilled water butt and emerged with a dripping expression of dogged determination.

He took stock of everything in the house, moving methodically from the loft to the cellar. He didn't say a word the whole time, which intrigued Alba, for her brothers or even her late father would have been swearing fair to colour the air with such strong language.

He finished just as the thatcher arrived to repair the roof, but he did not rest. No, he picked up a broom and swept every speck of soot out the back door, into the gutter. He cleaned the ash off his worktable before sweeping again. He looked like a priest sweeping the house of bad spirits.

She longed to tell him that he need not worry, for the only bad spirits about were those belonging to her brothers, and she suspected they'd sneaked into a neighbouring cellar in search of an even more troublesome kind of spirit. If it was true, they wouldn't return until they'd drained the contents of their neighbour's still, or they woke up from their alcohol-induced stupor. The longer they were gone, the better.

By noon, his house looked like the fire had never been, except for the scorch marks on the table and the burned remnants of his week's work sitting in a sad little pile on the scorched timber.

That's when Dagny arrived, sashaying into the house as though she owned the place. Alba wanted to slap the coy smile off the girl's face as she bent over to offer the shoemaker a sample of her cooking. Alba's rage simmered as the girl's breasts nearly spilled out of the front of her dress, she'd laced the gown so tight. And probably padded it, too, Alba fumed. Dagny had often bemoaned her flat chest on the Sundays she'd walked to church with Alba. The skinny girl was no plumper anywhere else, so her suddenly buxom chest must be the result of some artifice.

"Thank you," the shoemaker said, taking the food from her without more than a cursory glance.

Alba smiled viciously. He wasn't interested in Dagny.

"I'm sorry, but I don't know your name," the shoemaker continued.

Dagny blushed and cast her eyes down at her cleavage. "I'm Dagny, daughter to William the wine merchant next door."

The shoemaker's eyes darted to the door, and the house from whence Dagny had come. "I'm Brogan. Shoemaker. You must tell your father to come to me when he needs new boots."

Alba wanted to crow at the girl's dashed hopes. Boots for her father, indeed, when Dagny would rather he was thinking of her breasts. But she had his name now – Brogan. She wanted to say it aloud, to savour the taste of it on her tongue, but she didn't dare.

Brogan dismissed Dagny with scarcely a second glance, to Alba's satisfaction, and went back to his worktable. He picked through the pile of burned leather, using his knife to pry the pieces apart to see if any of the shoes were salvageable. But, piece by piece, he dropped the remains of his week's work into the pail at his feet.

As the pieces fell apart between his fingers,

then plopped down to fill the pail, Alba's tears welled again, and she couldn't seem to stop them. Brogan's stony expression as he emptied the pail outside only made her cry harder until it was all she could do to stifle the sobs so he wouldn't hear her.

Her brothers would pay for ruining him, she swore. How, she didn't know, but it would happen. If there were saints above and hell below, then there would be a reckoning.

Fifteen

Brogan finished the last of his food before he set out what leather remained. A small piece, perhaps enough for one shoe, but not for two. Unless they were really small…

He found some chalk – a miracle that it had survived the blaze – and drew an outline on the hide. A moment later, he scrubbed it off with his sleeve and tried again.

Over and over, he attempted to find a way to fit two shoes on the leather, but no matter what he tried, they would not fit. Brogan scrubbed at his eyes. If he'd owned enough coin to buy a cup of ale, he'd drown his sorrows in it in a moment.

But he had no coin, and only one tiny piece of leather that would not make a pair of anything worth selling.

Yet he tried, and tried again, for Brogan refused to give up. He would make a living here. He had to.

"And no pesky fire-bug poltergeist will stop me," he said aloud, glaring into the shadows that now filled the house.

Somehow, he hadn't noticed it growing dark. The thatcher had long since departed, leaving the repaired roof behind.

Brogan had no candles left – his last one had burned alongside the boots. No food, no light, no livelihood. He had one thing remaining to him – hope.

Hope was what sustained him as he ascended the ladder to the loft, praying aloud that the morning would bring brighter things. It couldn't get any worse.

Sixteen

Alba wasn't sure what manner of thing a poltergeist was, but her brothers deserved any and all insults for what they'd done to Brogan. She'd watched him all day, wishing there was something she could do, and now she was resolved.

There was no point to secrecy. If he knew of her brothers, she had no need to hide their presence any more. And if her brothers could make all the mischief they liked…maybe it was time she enjoyed herself, too.

She'd regarded the lovely piece of leather

with such longing as Brogan had marked it so many times she lost count. And when he went upstairs, leaving it uncut…her decision was made in a moment.

Alba slid down from the rafters and retrieved her box of tools, along with the last shoe she'd ever made. Half-made, she reminded herself, and it was a good thing, too, for she'd need to unmake it to trace around the pieces to make its fellow. A perfect pair, or as close to it as she could manage. It had been years since she'd practiced her craft, and she dreaded finding out what she had forgotten in that time.

Alba took a candle out of her toolbox, and lit it from the dying embers of the fire. She set the candle on the table, figuring the scorched timbers wouldn't mind a little wax on them.

The piece of leather Brogan had left her was the perfect size for the second shoe. She wiped away the scores of chalk makes he'd made and began to trace her own pattern. Hesitantly at first, then more confidently as the warm magic of making began to take hold. She breathed it in, wanting to laugh aloud out of sheer joy, but that would wake Brogan. And she wanted this too much to hand it over to him, or anyone.

Her shears were harder to handle, but still she managed to cut the pieces to her satisfaction. The needle moved like a dream in her nimble fingers, shaping a shoe out of the pieces. Giving the hide life once more. Now, to make it bloom.

She set her flower moulds on the hearth, where the still-glowing coals might warm them. Alba's hands shook as she took a cloth and wet the leather, preparing the rich red-brown bed for its very own garden as though it were life-giving soil itself, and not leather made from a beast long dead.

Alba measured the shoe she'd embellished so long ago, making sure she had the placement just right, before she laid a flower mould against the hide. She tapped it with her hammer, lightly at first, and then harder to make her mark. Flowers blossomed beneath her fingers, on one shoe and then the other, for the design she'd done so long ago was too simple for her tastes today. The borders needed a tiny vine twining around them, the leaves placed just so, which wove its way around to the heels of this pair of…dancing slippers, she decided. Not boots at all.

A few more cuts and the change was made. Some lady would show silk-clad ankles as she danced in these at court, at a ball the likes of which Alba would never attend. No matter, though. Alba was clumsy on her feet – all her grace lay in her fingers as she made the leather obey her every wish.

There. Shoes fit for a queen, once they were done, Alba told herself, standing back to admire them. But they were not yet done.

Her paint jars were dry as a desert, but a few drops of water revived them. The brushes were as soft as the day she'd first seen them, for they were untouched – a final gift from her father before his death. She could think of no more fitting project for virgin brushes than the most perfect pair of shoes she'd ever created.

The flowers would be white, with just a touch of yellow-gold in the centres, the better to stand out of the russet leather. The vines and leaves would need to be pale, too, so that the greenery might be seen.

Alba painted until the candle burned down to nothing, and she lacked the light to see. Only when she could not discern the difference between the colours did she lay down her brush. Her heart raced and her breath was shallow, as though she had run a great distance, instead of sitting at the table for hours unmoving. Yet she felt happier than she had in years. Exhilarated, that was the word, with a joy she'd never thought to feel again.

Was this how God had felt when he created the world, and surveyed his creation for the first time? Alba wanted to laugh at her own daring. It was sacrilege, surely, to compare herself to God. And yet...

Her creation was far humbler, to be worn on feet that touched the ground, belonging to a lady who was higher than Alba would ever be. She was no deity, just a shoemaker who loved her craft.

Carefully, Alba set the shoes on the window sill, so that they might catch the first of the morning light. When the sun rose, then she would finish the work she had begun.

In the meantime, she would emulate the

master shoemaker and get some sleep.

Alba packed her tools back in their box, consigning them to their new hiding place before she lay down beside them. She would rest for only a moment, she promised herself, as she lay back and closed her eyes.

Seventeen

A furious pounding woke Brogan, like the worst hangover he'd ever suffered. "Never drinking again," he mumbled.

"Hello, the shoemaker!" a voice shouted, and the pounding began again

It dawned on Brogan that the noise did not come from the inside of his head, but from the door of his house. No, the door of his shop, for what other shoemaker lived here?

"Coming!" Brogan shouted, scrambling down the ladder. He yanked the door open and yelped as the cold morning air hit him. He wrapped his frozen body in a cloak before he could properly focus on the man who stood on the threshold. A man whose fur-lined silk cloak put Brogan's coarse wool to shame. Brogan hesitated for only a moment before he bent in a deep bow. He didn't know the man's rank, but he was certain he was far higher than Brogan would ever be. "My lord," he said.

Brogan must have guessed right, for the man didn't correct him. Instead, he asked, "Are you the shoemaker?"

The shoemaker? Was he after the King's shoemaker? His heart sinking, Brogan managed to say, "I am a shoemaker, my lord. I make shoes and this is my workshop."

"Good. How much for those?"

Brogan raised his head to find the man stabbing a finger at the window sill. Where there couldn't be anything worth selling, Brogan knew, for he'd checked the burned remains twice before discarding them, and he still hadn't decided what to do with the remaining leather.

Yet the morning light cascaded through the window like manna from heaven itself, haloing a pair of slippers so brightly they seemed to glow gold. Slippers the like of which Brogan had never seen before in his life.

"Come on, man, I must have them. Name your price," the lord said impatiently.

Brogan thought quickly. He had no idea where they'd come from, but they were in his shop. Ergo, they belonged to him. "I leave it to my lord to decide their value."

A purse landed at his feet, heavier than the one Brogan had arrived here with, judging by the clink of it.

"If it is not enough, tell me when I return, for I will. Once my wife sees these, she will want me to commission a dozen more," the man said. He snatched up the pair of shoes, tucked them into the pocket of his cloak, and departed.

Brogan couldn't seem to close his mouth. He could, however, reach down and pick up the purse. He swore when he saw the contents were all silver – a fortune like he'd never known before. This was too much for a pair of shoes. He hurried into the street, hoping to catch the man, but he'd mounted his horse and headed up the hill toward the castle. Even as Brogan watched, the man passed through the gate and out of reach.

He tightened his grip on the coins. While it might seem like a dream – shoes and lords and commissions and other such things – the coins were real, and they represented the future. The future of his shop, his livelihood...his breakfast.

Brogan wouldn't have to go back to Gereon's house and incur Tihana's wrath at his return.

Instead, he could go buy more leather to make boots. He'd made his first sale.

Why, he could even afford a barrel of ale, something he might drink in the evening when the work was done.

Filled with new hope, Brogan walked on air as he headed out of the house to break his fast.

Eighteen

When Alba woke, her stiffness told her she'd slept too long. Way past dawn, she discovered, and well into the afternoon, judging by the light. And too late to finish her work on those shoes, for she could hear Brogan's voice speaking to someone in the workroom above.

Not Dagny, she prayed. Anyone but Dagny.

Alba made her way up to the rafters, where she might spy unseen on Brogan and his visitor.

"She wants a dozen pairs, all different colours, to match her gowns. She sent her dressmaker with samples of the silk, so that you will get the colours right, she says," a man Alba did not know said. Yet his voice sounded familiar.

She squinted, trying to imagine him less stout, and without the grey in his hair. Her father had served many courtiers, and this one had been unusually besotted with his young wife. So much so that he'd run errands for her himself. What had her name been? Bessa. No, Wesa, a girl with hair so pale it had seemed white. She'd had a penchant for embroidery, and on the few occasions when Alba had seen her so that her father might measure her feet, she hadn't been able to stop staring at the intricate embroidery on every one of the girl's gowns. Now she knew where she'd seen the design she'd fashioned on the shoes she'd started to make all those years ago and worked on last night – one of Wesa's gowns.

If this was her husband, then he was Lord Soma. And Alba had to hide the shoes before he saw them and recognised his wife's design.

Alba's gaze darted to the windowsill. Her heart sank when she saw it was empty – the shoes were gone.

Perhaps Brogan had hidden them already, she reasoned. But how would he know to do that? His nervous demeanour, the way he stammered through his responses to Lord Soma…he didn't know the man, had not done business with him before. Unless he'd met Lady Wesa without her husband – scandalous, but not impossible – he couldn't know that Lord Soma would insist upon showing the shoes to his wife.

"I haven't seen her smile like that since our wedding day," Soma continued. "And I haven't seen her smile at all since our son was born. If it will make her happy, she shall have whatever she wants. A hundred such shoes like the ones I bought this morning, if she must."

Shoes he bought this morning, Alba repeated silently. But there hadn't been any shoes for sale in the shop this morning. The only pair had been…

Her initial horrified shock bled into anger. Brogan hadn't hidden the missing shoes. No, he'd sold her half-finished work to Lord Soma, and pocketed the proceeds. He was as bad as her brothers.

Worse, maybe, for her brothers at least took care of her. This man, this stranger, had stolen her work and sold it.

For a moment, she considered jumping down from the rafters and demanding her shoes back. Then sanity returned, and she knew she could not. Perhaps she should let her brothers burn the house down – only this time, with him inside it. When they returned, she would put her proposal to them.

In the meantime, she seethed as she continued to eavesdrop on the two men. Lord Soma wanted more shoes like the ones she'd made, did he? Well, he wouldn't get them. She'd die before she lifted a finger to help a thief who stole her work and passed it off as his own. Instead, she'd see what he could do, without her moulds or her paints or her skills.

Yet as she watched, Lord Soma piled coins on the table – more than enough to pay for such things. Brogan could buy his own tools twice over. A master shoemaker like himself would probably do a better job, too.

She didn't want to hear any more. Instead,

she slunk back down to the cellar. For one blissful night, she'd created something wonderful that lit up her life. But it was time to retreat into the darkness once more, for not even Brogan needed her.

Nineteen

"You will have these done by the end of next week, yes?" Lord Soma asked. "If you don't, my wife may insist I send some of my retainers to kill you."

Brogan swallowed nervously, not sure if the man was serious or jesting. "Y-yes, my lord," he managed to say. "Next week."

"Good man." Lord Soma left.

Brogan stared at the silver coins on the table. More than thirty of them, so why did he feel he'd sold his soul?

He could make good boots, and good

shoes, too. The money before him would easily cover the cost of the best leather for this job. Why, if the woman wanted shoes covered in silk to match the colours of the scraps sitting like a stack of tiny handkerchiefs beside the coins, then she should have them.

But for the life of him, Brogan couldn't remember what was so remarkable about the shoes in the window this morning. Not for the first time, he wished he'd taken a longer look at them. Long enough to be able to copy whatever had caught Lord Soma's eye, and captivated his wife so.

He could worry about that later, he told himself. First, he needed to buy the leather, or he would never have the work done by next week. He calculated how much he would need, then worked it out again, just to be sure, before he ventured to the tanner down by the river for the materials.

Loaded down with leather, pigments, thread and tools to replace the ones that burned, he returned home with just enough time to make a start on perhaps one pair of shoes.

Casting his mind back to the shoes he'd

glimpsed in the sun that morning, he tried to sketch a pattern that matched his memory. Tried, and tried again.

"If only I still had those shoes! How can I make something again, when I never saw it the first time? Gah!" Brogan threw his chalk down on the table, where it cracked in two. His father would be ashamed of him, whining like a child. No commission was too hard. None.

But perhaps he was too tired, from all the work of cleaning his house yesterday. Tomorrow would be better, when he was fresh.

Nodding to himself, Brogan climbed up to the loft to retire.

Twenty

When Alba heard Brogan return, she crept upstairs to see what he'd bought. Lovely leather, she noticed with approval, and enough pigments to paint the cathedral. Her fingers itched to touch them, to examine the veritable rainbow of colours he'd laid carelessly on the table. Her breath caught in her throat at the sight of the beautiful blue – he had bought the true ultramarine she'd only seen in the cathedral, adorning the Blessed Virgin's robes.

For the first time in her life, Alba felt lust. Or was it covetousness? But she didn't care what the sin was called. She wanted to grind that blue, mix it until it coated her brush just right, and paint…what? The skies on a shoe, so that the owner danced in clouds. Or should it be stars?

She dreamed of what she'd create with those glorious colours as Brogan laid out the leather and worked.

By the time he retired for the night, her anger at him had ebbed away completely, replaced by the irresistible desire to improve on the shoes she'd made last night. And seeing as Brogan had sold them to Lord Soma, she would create another pair from his leather, and apply colour with his paints.

In the end, she made two pairs of shoes, as alike and as different as day and night, for that's what they would be, she decided. One to match the deep blue silk sample, and another with creamy white clouds to be worn with the white.

She lit one candle, then another, for Brogan had bought a whole box of them, and she needed the light to work by. The clouds in her summery sky were simple enough, but she set them aside to let the paint dry a little before finishing the sky with that beautiful blue. Time to work on the night sky instead.

But which stars to paint?

Alba crept to the window and unshuttered it. She gasped as the winter cold engulfed her. One look at the sky, and then she could go and sit by the fire, she promised herself. Yet when she looked up, there was little to see. Every house in town had stoked their fires to warm them through the night, and the smoke was so thick it formed a cloud over the city. She couldn't see a single star – she didn't even know if the moon was out tonight.

Dejected, Alba fastened the shutters and went to the fire to warm herself. It took some time before feeling returned to her bare toes, but by then, she'd made her decision. The Lyra constellation, the one her father had shown her on clear summer nights, saying it was bright in the sky on the night she was born. It would turn into a beautiful design over the toes of each shoe, and she'd put a smattering of smaller stars, pinpricks, really, around the rest of them.

She took out her tools and laid them to warm on the hearth. This time, she would finish the job before she went to sleep, she swore.

The candle burned down as she turned ordinary leather into glimmering firmament. Alba was breathless when she finally set the second shoe down, but the smile wouldn't leave her lips. These night sky shoes were better than yesterday's design. When Lady Wesa wore these, she would truly be dancing on air.

Alba washed her brushes carefully before she turned back to the clouds. The sky here must be lighter, less brilliant. A watery blue, almost white, but bright enough to contrast with the clouds. There was more skill to the paint and the brush strokes on this pair, for there was no embossing to guide her.

Yet when she was done, Alba was proud of these, too. Two pairs of summer skies, midday and midnight, lay on the table in the candlelight.

Perhaps another coat of that blue…

Her brothers' unmistakeable voices sounded

from the cellar. They were home, and drunk.

Alba blew out the candle and flew down the stairs to greet them, hoping to get them to bed before they saw her handiwork.

The cellar smelled like they'd finished off the still, and Gad slurred his words so badly, Alba suspected they had. Sleeping this off would take them days. Days they would be too busy in bed to make mischief for her or Brogan.

She breathed a sigh of relief and busied herself in getting her brothers into bed. She didn't dare return to the workroom tonight. Tomorrow, perhaps.

Twenty-One

When Brogan climbed down the ladder this time, there was no one banging on the door, and there were shoes on the table. He had to rub his eyes twice to make sure he wasn't seeing things.

No, they were still there. Two pairs of shoes, each pair a different shade of blue, looking more like works of art than something a woman would wear on her feet. Brogan walked around the table, taking them in from every angle. Never in his wildest dreams could he create something like this. Oh, sure, he could fashion the shoes well enough – the workmanship of these was fine, but now he could see them, he could match it. Whatever had been done with the paint, though…not even the art in the new cathedral compared to it. So small and detailed, yet so perfect. He picked up one of the shoes covered in clouds. Yes, there was a tiny bird winging its way through the sky. How had anyone been able to paint something so small, yet so perfectly?

As Brogan's brain began to wake up, bigger questions came to mind. Not how, but who. And why.

Who had done this? If it was the ghost that had tried to burn his house down, why was it painting now? Some sort of penance? It didn't make sense.

Tentatively, he reached for the nearest pair of shoes. They sat on his hand, a reassuringly real weight. However ghostly their creator might be, the slippers were as real as the leather he'd bought yesterday.

And with these in his hand, he had all he needed to make as many as Lord Soma liked. Enough for every lady in court, if it came to it.

Brogan set the shoes on the windowsill where he could see them and pulled a fresh hide onto the table. He'd cut the pieces for three pairs of shoes before his growling stomach reminded him he hadn't eaten since last night.

He stuck his head outside and beckoned to one of the boys playing in the street. "Two coppers for you if you go to the nearest bakery and bring me some breakfast." He handed the boy some money and went back to work.

The boy returned with a basket of bread and cakes, wearing a big grin. Brogan paid him and the boy scampered off.

Brogan munched on the nearest cake as he examined the shoes in the window once more. The stitches were so small he'd have trouble copying them. These weren't the work of a man, that was certain. Unless ghosts had smaller hands in death than they'd had in life…

Brogan shook his head and set the shoe down.

A feminine giggle sounded in the street. "Aren't those the prettiest shoes ever made? How much for them?"

It took Brogan a moment to realise the girl had addressed him. "I'm afraid these are already sold, mistress. But perhaps I could make some more for you." He named the price Lord Soma had offered him for the shoes.

The older woman standing behind the giggling girl, presumably her mother, shook her head. Then the bargaining began.

Brogan had haggled in his father's shop often enough, so this part of the business came easily to him. Even if the prices were much higher. They settled for a sum that made his head spin. Why, he would make his fortune within the year, at this rate. Maybe not shoemaker to the King, but shoemaker to half the court, if he could manage it.

He told the ladies to return in two weeks for their commission, writing it down in his ledger below the order from Lord Soma.

Then he went back to work.

Several times throughout the day he was forced to return to his ledger, as every lady who passed his window wanted to enquire after the shoes, and half of them insisted upon buying a pair. Business had never been so brisk for Brogan – not even in his father's shop. Perhaps his fortunes really were changing.

Twenty-Two

"But I simply MUST have them, Mister Brogan!" a shrill voice cried.

The voice belonged to a woman who looked old enough to be Brogan's mother, but from the way she simpered at him, she didn't have maternal instincts in mind.

"I can put you down for a pair in three weeks' time, mistress, but I'm all booked up until then. I'll need to find an assistant as it is," Brogan said, his quill poised above the ledger. "What will it be?"

The woman's eyes darted to the starry shoes

on the windowsill – Alba's work from last night, she realised, though with less of a jolt than she expected. He hadn't sold her shoes, but he had promised what looked like several similar pairs to customers over the course of the day. Clever man.

He'd be a rich man, too, if today was any indication. Her father hadn't commanded such a high price, and he'd made shoes for the King.

Brogan concluded his deal with the woman and ushered her out, closing the door behind him.

Only when Alba was certain he'd gone did she dare to leave her hiding place to look more closely at his ledger. No wonder he wanted an assistant. So many shoes…not even if he worked day and night would he be able to meet these orders and Lord Soma's.

Would his assistant cut and sew the shoes, or paint the designs?

Alba's heart froze. They were her designs, no one else's. Brogan's customers today had fallen in love with her work, not some stranger's imitation of it.

Brogan had made four pairs of slippers

today, in between filling his ledger with orders. Four pairs for Lady Wesa, for her order came first.

Alba stroked the topmost piece of silk, pinned to the ledger page. A wine-coloured gown, one that reminded her of roses. Red flowers would be hard to paint on the leather Brogan had bought, for it was almost the same shade of red.

That would be his problem to solve, she told herself. Not hers. He had sold the shoes, so he must make them.

Using the lovely pigments she'd played with last night…

No.

He had bought the materials, Alba reasoned, and it wasn't like she had anything better to do. And wouldn't it be lovely to know that court ladies – real ladies – wore her designs once more, and loved them as much as she did?

No. He'd sold her shoes. Hers.

Not that Lord Soma had given him much choice. And he'd promptly gone out and bought more leather and paint to make more. Countless more.

Alba was so busy arguing with herself in her own head that she didn't notice the heavy footsteps approaching the door until it swung open. With a muffled squeak, she ducked under the worktable, hoping it was too dark for him to see her in the shadows.

She held her breath as Brogan hung up his cloak, humming, before he approached the table. His shoes were inches from her.

"Tomorrow, I get to try my hand at painting, though heaven knows how I'll make these look like that," Brogan said. "If there are any helpful ghosts listening, I would pay almost any price for your help again. You know how to make shoes fit for court better than I."

She did? Alba wanted to laugh. Brogan thought she was better than him?

"Tell me what you need, or write it down. I will see that you get it. More colours, finer thread, anything. Just don't burn my house down while I sleep, for I've had one ale too many tonight, I fear, and I plan to sleep like the dead."

Brogan kicked off his boots and climbed up

to the loft. A soft thump told Alba he'd retired for the night.

She stayed under the table until she heard faint snoring from upstairs. Then she knew she was safe to come out.

The house fire. It hadn't been her fault, but it had been her brothers'. Her family owed him a debt, for the fire had nearly cost him everything he had.

"I will help you, Brogan," she said softly, tasting his name on her tongue for the first time. It felt strangely right.

Twenty-Three

Brogan held his breath as he descended from the loft this time. He didn't think he'd find more masterpieces, but, oh, how he hoped.

On the table sat the same eight shoes he'd left there last night…transformed from base leather into something divine. The toes of one pair had been embossed and painted so cunningly that it looked like a full-blown rose lay atop each shoe. He had to touch them to be sure the lifelike roses were not truly there. Marvellous.

Yellow flowers twined around another pair,

much like the first pair he remembered seeing, but these were bigger, bolder. Their vines twined around the rest of the shoe, but the flowers on the toes seemed to shout for attention. He couldn't remember the previous pair doing that.

Another had berries instead of flowers, peeping through the leaves as though waiting to be plucked. Each pair of painted shoes sat beside a piece of silk that matched the paint colours perfectly. He glanced at the window, where the blue silk pieces sat beside their shoes. Six done, six more to go, plus the boots, he worked out, checking his ledger.

A sheet had been torn out of the book, and a meticulous hand had written:

You will need white leather, and some in yellow-gold, and some more of that ultramarine pigment for the night sky shoes. Another of those cakes filled with jam, too, if you please. Painting is hungry work, and I ate yours.

Brogan laughed aloud. A ghost who ate cakes. What next?

No, a ghost who had saved him, and made

shoes fit for angels.

"You shall have all this and more," Brogan promised. He sent one of the street boys for breakfast, then decided to send him to buy leather and pigments, too. He had too much work to do to traipse around town, picking up supplies.

Slippers took shape beneath his fingers, only to be laid down on the table when another customer stopped to admire the rose shoes in the window. He had a dozen more orders before noon, and still they kept coming.

But when evening came, he shut the shop, and lined up the day's finished shoes on the table, knowing with a certainty he couldn't explain that the helpful ghost would return and work its magic once more. He even laid the last jam dumpling-cake beside the shoes, as an offering to his own personal saint. But which saint?

Saint Crispin, the patron saint of shoemakers, had survived a fire meant to kill him. Perhaps it was him. What Brogan had done to deserve this most holy saint's attention, he did not know, but he was more grateful than words could say.

Twenty-Four

"What are you doing?" Gad asked at Alba's elbow. He stuck a finger in the paint she'd carefully mixed to just the right shade on her palette. "Where'd you get this stuff?"

She smacked his hand away. "They belong to the shoemaker who lives here. I'm helping him."

"Why?" Onni whined.

She thought for a moment, knowing her brothers wouldn't understand her desire to create something beautiful. When had they ever created anything?

Finally, she said, "Because burning the house down didn't break the curse. We're still stuck here, aren't we? I thought I might try another way. If we help him, he might be so grateful that he'd be willing to help us break the curse."

Gad snorted. "Or he might just get so used to having his own personal slave, that he'll never set us free. Would you want to lose an elf who comes in the night, does all your work, and never needs to be paid for it?"

The beaming smiles of Brogan's customers as they bore their purchases out his shop — shoes she had created — made her brave. Alba lifted her chin. "No one can do the work I do." She set a mould against the leather and tapped it gently with her hammer.

"What, paint flowers?" Onni mocked. He picked up a brush and, before Alba could stop him, swiped it across the toes of an unpainted shoe. "Seems pretty simple to me."

Fury bubbled up in Alba, with a force she'd never known before. She slammed the hammer down on her brother's fingers. "If you ever think to do that again, I will wait until you are asleep, and the next thing I hit with this hammer will be your head. Until there is not a brain left to think anything ever again."

Onni stuck his fingers in his mouth and looked hurt. "You're a real shrew, sis. Good thing we saved the men of this town from marrying you."

"Call me what you like, but if you damage anything else in this shop, either of you, the last thing you will ever feel is my hammer," Alba threatened.

"Let's go, Onni," Gad said, tugging on his brother's arm. "Let our shrew of a sister waste her time however she likes. We'll be better served by emptying that still before Christmas."

"Good riddance," Alba muttered as she smoothed a damp cloth across the leather, erasing the mark Onni had made. No one painted shoes in this workshop but her. She didn't care about the curse any more – as long as she could paint, her life was complete. Who cared about husbands and marriage, anyway? She didn't need them.

The only man she wanted was Brogan, and

that was because he made her shoes and bought her paint. Hardly something a husband would do.

Twenty-Five

Every day, Brogan cobbled shoes together and took more orders than he could make from lords and ladies he wouldn't have had the temerity to speak to before.

And every night, Alba transformed his handsome shoes into works of art. No two pairs were the same, as no two flowers were the same, and the pictures that formed beneath her brush took on a life of their own.

Alba's brothers ignored her, as they usually did, preferring instead to steal from their neighbours' stills. They'd drained one, but found another, and they'd made it their mission to make sure no one had spirits left in their cellars by Christmas.

But Christmas was coming, as evidenced by the number of new commissions Brogan accepted every day. New shoes to wear to mass, for the new year, for this party and that. Gifts for wives and daughters, mistresses and maidens the men hoped might become more, in time. Wealthy merchants came to his door, too, hearing of how ladies wore his shoes at court and wanting the same for their wives at home.

In the new year, Brogan would take an apprentice, he promised himself. Someone who could cut out the shoes and take the orders while he worked. When he wasn't too busy to teach anyone anything.

Without his mysterious nightly visitor, Brogan would never have been able to meet the demand. Every time he put more coins into his strongbox – he'd had to buy a strongbox, then another – he thanked his saintly benefactor.

But every morning, his curiosity grew

stronger. He wanted to see the miracle, not merely the result of it.

Yet every evening when he was tempted to hide in the workroom instead of heading up to bed, he reminded himself that it would be sacrilege to ask the saints to show him their miracles. Worse, if he saw them, would the miracles stop?

Not wanting to bring bad luck on himself, Brogan forced himself up the ladder, every night.

Until one day, Drogo, the street boy who had become his personal errand-boy, came in with a basket of cakes from the baker in the middle of the afternoon.

"I didn't send for these," Brogan said. He still had the basket from this morning, containing the jam cake he'd place on the table before he went to bed, as he did every night, knowing it would be gone by morning.

"It's a Yuletide gift from the baker, Master Brogan," Drogo said proudly. He grinned, and only now did Brogan notice the jam smeared across his face. "He gave me a cake, too, as thanks for the business."

Thanks for…if Brogan owed anyone thanks, it was his night-time visitor. A cake seemed poor payment for such exquisite work.

Tonight, Brogan resolved, he would stay awake and keep watch for his mysterious saint. Then, if he dared, he would ask how to repay him.

Twenty-Six

One or both of her brothers had drunk so much they'd brought it all back up again. Alba could smell the bile when she woke, and it turned her stomach. "What is it about you boys and bodily fluids?" she grumbled as she got up to clean up the mess.

Onni and Gad denied they'd made the mess, and each tried to blame the other. Loudly.

If they weren't careful, Brogan would hear them and come down to the cellar to investigate. And, despite all the work she'd done for him, she wasn't yet ready to reveal herself to him.

"Can you go and see if the shoemaker is still up working?" she asked.

"Only because the air's better up there," Onni grumbled, heading up the steps, with Gad not far behind.

Alba muttered under her breath about the uselessness of men, and her brothers in general, as she cleaned up their mess. Then she drew a bucket of water from the well and washed thoroughly until she was sure she didn't smell of vomit any more.

Only then did she venture upstairs, to find four pairs of shoes waiting for her, and no sign of her brothers at all. No matter. She shrugged them off, and set to work.

Twenty-Seven

"Time for bed," Brogan said loudly, feeling like a fool. He added an extra log to the fire, muttering to himself about how he hoped it would be enough with the nights so cold, for he didn't want to wake up and find the fire gone out. Only then did he climb up to the loft.

But instead of lying on his pallet, he stretched out by the top of the ladder, where he had a clear view of most of the workroom. The empty workroom.

Brogan sighed, resting his head on his arms

as his vigil grew tedious. What if nothing happened, and no one came? A saint would know he was watching. A saint would also condemn him for his deceit.

This was a bad idea, and he should go to bed like he'd said he would. No one was coming, now or ever. He'd done the unforgivable, and now —

Faint sounds reached him, like footsteps on the wooden floor below.

Brogan leaned forward, eagerly.

A crash, followed by swearing.

Brogan choked back a laugh. He didn't think saints swore.

"Light a bloody candle before I trip over anything else," a male voice grumbled.

Light blossomed near the fire, outlining a man's shadow against the wall.

It was Saint Crispin, Brogan thought excitedly.

The candle finally came into view on the table, but Brogan couldn't see the hand holding it. Then he did, and his mouth fell open.

It was a man, all right — a tiny man maybe

two feet high, who had to climb onto the table to examine the shoes laid out there. He lifted one in his hands. "This is fine work."

"What would you know of fine work?" another voice grumbled, and a second man climbed onto the table beside the first. "The shoes I made were always better than yours, but you denied it!"

"That's because that's a lie. The worst boot ever made was better than your best!"

The two men squared up on the tabletop, as if ready to fight each other.

Only then did Brogan realise they were completely naked – not a stitch of clothing between them. How did they endure the cold?

It must be magic, he decided. For the men rolling around under the table punching each other and shouting curses could not be saints. They must be elves, magical creatures he'd heard tales of but never seen. Such small hands could paint tiny details on shoes that Brogan himself would never manage

He'd never heard of them not wearing clothes, though.

And he had his answer of how to thank

them.

On the morrow, he would go to a tailor, and have him make clothes for the two men. A suit each, and he would make boots to match. A fitting Christmas thank-you gift for the men who had helped to make his fortune.

Happy, Brogan stretched out on his pallet and drifted off into a dream.

Twenty-Eight

"I hope your nephews like them," the tailor said eagerly as he set out the finished items. "Two pairs of hose, two undershirts, two tunics, and two cloaks to cover them when they play in the snow." He smiled and laid two hats on the table. "And my wife made these for them. We have no children of our own, see, and she thought it would be a fitting gift."

Awkwardly, Brogan thanked the tailor and his wife for their kindness. He'd paid them plenty for the clothes, of course, and more to make them as quickly as possible. He hoped the two elves liked the gift, and it didn't drive them away, for they would know he'd seen them.

Yet he couldn't, in conscience, profit from their kindness any more without giving them something in return.

So later that night, when he'd lined up today's finished shoes on the table, he also laid out the clothes. And added a final touch – the two pairs of tiny boots he'd made, hoping he'd judged their measurements correctly.

Then he crept up to the loft to watch, and wait.

He didn't have to wait long.

"Four pairs again today," one of the men said. "You going to tell her, or shall I?"

"She'll find out for herself, soon enough," the other said. A sharp intake of breath. "Look at this, Gad. Clothes."

A snort. "You sound like you've never seen clothes before, Onni. I remember when you used to wear them, before the curse and all. Maybe the curse has addled your wits."

One of the men climbed onto the bench. "Not like this. These are in our size. Could they be for us?"

"What are you talking about?" The second man – Gad? – climbed onto the table. "By God's left nut, you're right. The little shrew was right for once." He seized the nearest pair of hose. "Quick, put them on!"

They dressed with all the haste of men caught in the bedchamber of another man's wife, when the rightful husband returned home. Before they'd even properly gotten their boots on, they ran outside, whooping and cheering as though they'd won a tourney. Brogan could hear them carrying on for some time, before they fell silent or moved out of earshot.

He waited, but they didn't return, so he decided to get some sleep, happy in the thought that his gifts had been well received. He was no longer in their debt.

Twenty-Nine

Once again, by the time Alba was done cleaning up the cellar and then herself, her brothers had vanished. They'd agreed to go upstairs eagerly enough…what had she asked them to do again? Oh, that's right. She'd asked them to tell her how many shoes she had to paint, though she knew Brogan rarely made more than four pairs in a day, which she could easily manage to paint in a night. It had been the first thing that came to mind to get them out of her way, so that she could clean up more quickly.

Though why she bothered any more, she wasn't sure. The cellar smelled almost permanently of vomit, no matter what she did. The sooner her brothers emptied that still, the better. Though they'd probably just find another one and steal the contents of that.

So there would be no end to a life of endless drudgery, slave to her brothers, with no light in sight. Perhaps burning alive might have been a better fate, after all.

But there was one light, even if she only did it in darkness. Her painting. She would endure an eternity of drudgery if her nights were her own to paint until the sun rose.

Alba's tread was light as she almost skipped up the steps to the workroom. Her brothers were gone, as usual, but the shoes were waiting. Along with all the pigments she could ever want.

She was running low on that blue, though. Alba opened the ledger and made a note for Brogan to order more ultramarine. Half the city seemed to want a night sky full of stars on their feet for Christmas, and who was she to blame them? If she could wear shoes, she would want to dance among the stars, too. But her toes would be bare until the day she died, unless by some miracle someone broke the curse.

A tear trickled down her cheek, but Alba wiped it away. She had shoes aplenty, even if she couldn't wear them. And tonight's shoes would wear the swan constellation, or perhaps the bear.

She set her moulds to warm by the fire while she prepared her paints, as she did every night. Embellishing took next to no time tonight, which meant more time to paint.

Tonight, the skies on her shoes would have a hint of purple to them, she decided, adding a pinch of vermillion. But the stars would be white, without a hint of yellow. It was winter, after all, and the air smelled of snow.

But inside, the shoe-skies were clear enough to see all the stars.

At least, they were until a man's voice demanded, "What in heaven's name are you doing to my shoes?"

Thirty

A tinkling sound woke Brogan, like tools falling to the floor. Ah, his elven shoemakers were back. Burning with curiosity to see them at work, he shuffled over to the edge of the loft and peered down. He saw no one at first, but the tinkling sounds continued, so he told himself to be patient.

Then it seemed the fire moved from the grate to hover in the air beside the table, and Brogan's voice died in his throat even as he tried to shout a warning. He'd almost lost his house through fire once; he would not lose it again now, when things were going to so well.

But it wasn't fire at all, not really, he realised as his eyes told him an impossible tale.

The brown sack the elf girl wore was the same colour as the wood of the floor or his table, so he hadn't seen her until she moved. Her flame-red hair, though, was something else entirely. It seemed to have a life of its own, which is why he'd initially thought he was staring at fire.

Then she picked up the shoe.

Visions of her destroying his work like she'd tried to destroy his house spurred Brogan into action. He scrambled down the ladder, shouting, "What in heaven's name are you doing to my shoes?"

The shoe dropped.

Her voice was soft and expressionless. "Painting them." She reached for a brush and dipped it delicately in a pot of paint.

Brogan edged around the table, wanting, nay, needing to see her face. If this tiny elf was the reason for all his misfortunes, then by all that was holy, he would look her in the eye as he berated her for them.

But she didn't raise her head to look at him. She was too intent on the shoe, stroking her brush across them as lovingly as Tihana stroked Gereon's…Brogan swallowed. He didn't want to think about his brother and his wife right now.

Not with his shop at stake.

He watched her for a few minutes, without saying a word. Then, finally, he said, "How do you do that?"

Her eyebrows rose. "Paint the shoes? The same as you would, I imagine. I mix the paints, then take a brush, dip it into the paint and put it on the shoe." She demonstrated, but the way she handled the brush was far more sensuous than her matter-of-fact tone.

Brogan set his hands on the table to steady himself. The elf girl was working some sort of magic on him. He was certain of it. "No, when I do it, it looks flat. Like when I whitewashed the walls outside. Yet when you do it, I see the sky. With stars."

Or flowers. Or leaves. Or vines that seem to come to life. Realisation dawned that he was looking at the person who had painted not just this shoe, but everything.

He sat down heavily on the bench across from her. "The flower shoes. Those were yours. And…every…shoe…since…"

The tip of the brush glided into the paint and vanished, like a candle wick into hot, molten wax. "I made the first pair, yes. But you made the shoes. I merely painted them." The brush withdrew, dripping, before it rolled across the glorious curves of the shoe she cradled in her hand.

He shifted uncomfortably. His hose should not feel this tight. Perhaps the washerwoman had shrunk them.

"I thought it was an angel, or some sort of saint," he blurted out before he could stop himself.

As he'd feared, she laughed. The sound tinkled like church bells at a wedding. "My painting made you think of angels?"

"It's beautiful," he defended himself. Like you, he almost said before he clamped his mouth shut.

A smile blossomed on her face, and she raised her eyes to meet his. Ultramarine, he thought. The same as the pigment she used so much. He'd need to buy more again soon, so she wouldn't run out.

"Thank you," she said. She dropped her gaze to the table. "No one has ever liked my work before."

"You must be joking. The whole city is mad for it. I can't take orders fast enough to satisfy them, and the prices they pay for it…I could not afford such shoes, and yet I sell a dozen or more every day." Brogan smacked his fist into the table. "And to think I believed those two men made such beautiful things. When it's you…you…" He gestured at the finished shoe she'd set on the table.

Up went those eyebrows again. "What men?"

"Elves, like you," Brogan said, instantly regretting it. The other two were nothing like her. Maybe the same height, but that's where the similarity ended. Men were men, while she was…enchanting.

She nodded, as though she understood. "You have seen my brothers, then." She didn't sound particularly enthused by this.

"Well, briefly, yes," he admitted. "They took the clothes I'd had made for them, and they left."

Her shoe thumped to the table. "You gave them clothes? No wonder they did not return. You broke the curse and set them free. They will not be back, unless they come to collect something they left behind."

Brogan glimpsed despair in her eyes that matched the bitterness in her tone before she returned to her work. Her brush strokes were soothing now, easing away pain.

"Not even you, their sister?" he asked quietly.

Tears welled in her eyes and fell. "No. Least of all me. I am worthless to them."

Thirty-One

Alba sniffled, wiping away her tears before she dared meet Brogan's eyes again. After watching him for so long, talking to him seemed the most natural thing in the world. But now, he was the one watching her. Her hands, at least, as she painted his shoes. Perhaps he didn't quite trust her to do it right, which was fair. He didn't know her, after all. But that hungry look in his eyes as he stared at her hands, as though he was hungry for something more than food. That look…warmed her insides in the strangest way.

"My brothers call me a shrew, and perhaps they are right. All I wish to do is paint, and they make messes that I must clean up, which takes me away from what I love," she admitted.

"With skills like yours, you could make a fortune. More than enough to employ a maid to do that sort of work," Brogan said.

Alba laughed softly. "I cannot. It is part of the curse, after all. To work, and work, and work, and never be paid for it. Until someone frees us, like you did for my brothers." Her laughter turned bitter. "I believe this is called irony. Those lazy fools never did a day's work in their lives, yet you freed them without a thought."

Brogan bridled at the accusation. "I thought plenty, I assure you. I thought they had decorated all the shoes my customers bought, and I wanted to thank them. They were naked, and it was so cold...how could I let anyone go naked in this weather? Especially someone I owe so much." He stared at her a second, then amended, "Someone I thought I owed much. Evidently I was mistaken."

She couldn't bring herself to be angry at Brogan. She truly couldn't. "You thought you were doing them a kindness. You are a kind man. You weren't to know..." She paused, wondering if there was some shred of family loyalty left that made her hold her tongue.

Brogan pounced. "Know what?"

She had no loyalty to brothers who had deserted her. "They lit the fire that burned your house," she admitted. "While you slept, they would undo your work, or hide your tools. They wanted you to leave." Not for the first time, she wished she had been able to stop them, but her brothers had never listened to her.

"And what about you?" Brogan asked sharply.

Alba hung her head. "When you sold my shoes, that first pair with the flowers, I thought to steal your paints, and some leather to replace them. But my brothers distracted me before the paint was dry, and I left you the stars." She gestured at the finished pair of shoes before her. "Like this, but with the lyre, not the bear."

Brogan nodded. "I remember. With a single pair of shoes, you drove a whole city mad for stars. I will forever be in your debt. If there is anything I can do for you, anything at all…" He swallowed. "Name it, and I shall make it yours."

"Clothes." Alba's throat was so dry, her voice was scarcely audible. She cleared her throat and said it again. "Clothes. A gown and an underdress, some stockings, and shoes. Nothing like as rich as what they wear at court. Something simple, befitting a shoemaker's daughter. But it must be made for me, and given freely as a gift, in order to break the curse."

"And then you will be free?" Brogan asked.

Alba bowed her head. "Yes. Then I will be free."

Thirty-Two

"On the morrow, I will return to the tailor, and ask for all of those things," Brogan promised her, and was rewarded with another of her smiles. He didn't even know her name. "Please, what can I call you? Mistress Elf does not seem right."

More tinkling laughter. "I am not an elf, merely a human cursed to work like one. I am not sure real elves exist. My mother and father called me Alba."

"Alba," he repeated. He'd heard that before, somewhere. No, seen it. "Like the…"

She blushed. "The letters I carved into the table with my father's shears. Yes. Not even the fire managed to burn that away. I carved it on the day my father told me I could never inherit his shop – my brothers, who hated work and would do anything to get out of doing it – would inherit the place I loved most, while I would be too busy looking after my husband to make shoes, he said. But he died before he could find me someone suitable, and left me with my useless brothers instead. Brothers who sold everything they could, including the shoes I made, though I don't know what they did with the money. They certainly didn't pay the rent. When the landlord evicted us, they turned to banditry. Robbing travellers on the road to town. They made me tend their fire and cook for them, until they realised I would make a fine distraction. They'd leave me in the road, a maiden in distress, to be rescued by whatever traveller came past. While everyone was busy tending to me, they'd rob them blind." Alba's expression grew bitter. "They gave me little choice in the matter. It was do as I was told, or they would sell me like everything else. One night when he'd drunk too much, Onni let slip how much his favourite whorehouse was willing to pay for me, too. And it is less than you charge for a pair of painted shoes."

Her brothers had tried to sell her to a whorehouse? Now, more than ever, Brogan's anger burned at the brothers, who he'd inadvertently set free. And at himself, for being so stupid.

"They deserved the curse," he found himself saying.

"They did not find it much of a curse," Alba replied, taking up her brush again. Her rhythmic strokes seemed to punctuate her tale. "Their small stature made it easier for them to sneak inside places to steal things, and stay unseen. They could get drunk on much less wine, or whatever it was they drank. I never did find out whose still they stole from. As for work, they never did a lick of it before the curse, and they did even less after. And they did not miss clothes, for the curse ensured we were never cold."

Once again, Brogan stared at her sack.

"Why do you wear that, then? If you don't need to wear clothes."

A rosy blush coloured Alba's cheeks. "I may have lost everything else, but I still have a little dignity, and some modesty. My brothers may have wanted to sell me to a whorehouse, but I am no whore, sir."

Brogan stumbled over himself to apologise for insulting her. Just the thought of this beautiful woman, forced to sell her body, made him furious.

"Tomorrow, I will buy you a gown to replace what you have lost," Brogan swore. "And should your brothers return, I will defend you."

He dug out some of the leather he'd cut for tomorrow, and set up his tools across the table from her. While she painted, he would work, too. And if he worked a little slower than usual, could anyone blame him? He shared a workroom with the most beautiful woman he'd ever seen, albeit the smallest one, too, and she worked magic he could barely believe.

Thirty-Three

Brogan woke to someone knocking at his door. He raised his head blearily from the table, taking a moment to realise he hadn't slept in the loft, before he stumbled to greet his first customer of the morning.

No, the first customer of the afternoon, he realised in horror as he took in how high the sun hung in the sky. Nevertheless, he recovered quickly, ushering the merchant's wife into his workroom to measure her feet.

A steady stream of customers followed, giving him scarcely a moment to muse on what he'd learned last night from the elfin woman named Alba. Who was nowhere to be seen now, but her neat row of painted shoes told him he had not imagined her.

Like every other day since the first pair of painted slippers had graced his windowsill, he took orders for more shoes than he could make, and everyone wanted it before Christmas, only days away. Yet even when he told them they wouldn't have their order until the new year, still they agreed to his terms. There was something magical about Alba's shoes, as much as there was about Alba herself.

He could scarcely wait for the day to end so that he might see her again.

"A busy day for you, Brogan." Her soft voice was at his side before he'd realised it.

Brogan glanced at the window, surprised to discover that it was dark as pitch outside. "Where did the day go?"

She scaled the windowsill and bolted the shutters. "'Tis Midwinter, and the shortest day of the year. It is never long enough to do all that you must, I find."

All that he must… Brogan's heart sank. "I forgot to order your clothes," he said. "I'm sorry, Alba. Tomorrow…" But tomorrow would be just as busy, he was certain of it.

The smile she gave him was sad. The men in her life had disappointed her many times — what was one more? it seemed to say.

All the more reason not to be one of them, Brogan swore. "I will have them for you by Christmas, if I have to sew the damn things myself."

She laughed. "A leather gown would be very warm, but I would prefer linen or wool for the underdress. They would not chafe so."

The thought of anything chafing her delicate skin made him feel unusually warm. "As you wish." He eyed the sack she wore which looked uncommonly like the one Tihana had packed his food in when he had first arrived. "Anything to get you out of that dreadful sack."

She blushed, and Brogan realised what he'd said, too late. He stammered an apology, but she cut him short.

"I know you didn't get much made today.

Send for some dinner, and we can work together while you wait for it," she said.

Drogo had gone home to his parents for the day, so Brogan headed down the road to rap at his door. Drogo was just finishing his own dinner, and he was happy to run another errand or two, he said.

"Then I have a special commission for you, and you must remember it exactly," Brogan said. "You must go to the tailor who made clothes for my nephews, and tell him that I was wrong, for one of the children is a niece. He must make her two gowns to the same measurements, with all the suitable underthings, in blue. One is to be the shade of the summer sky, and the other is to be the same as the ultramarine pigment you bring me for the shoes with stars. And I must have these before the sun sets on Christmas Eve."

Drogo's eyes grew wide. "In two days? What if he says no, sir?"

Brogan would not break his word to Alba. "Tell him I will pay whatever it costs. Whatever I must. I will make his wife shoes fit for the Queen herself if only he will do this for me."

Drogo nodded. "I understand, sir."

"And when you've done that, bring me some dinner from the tavern," Brogan said. "Enough for two, I think. All this work and cold weather makes a man hungry."

Drogo grinned. "That's what my mother says, sir." He ran off into the dark, promising to do everything he was asked.

Brogan believed him. He had to, for he knew there was no other way he could keep his promise to Alba.

Thirty-Four

Brogan appeared relieved about something when he returned. Probably the imminent arrival of his dinner, Alba guessed. She was partway through cutting the pieces for a shoe.

"I should be doing that, not you," Brogan exclaimed, reaching for her shears.

"You can do the next pair. These shears are mine. Besides, I bet you'll still finish yours first, because your bigger hands can sew faster," she said.

"I never met a girl willing to wager before," Brogan said.

Alba managed a smile. "Living with my brothers has taught me many bad habits. If I am to rejoin the world again, I will have to unlearn them, I suppose."

"I see nothing that needs changing," Brogan said. "And I realised today, you never did tell me how you came to be cursed. Will you tell me the tale while we work?"

"If you want to hear it." At Brogan's nod, Alba continued, "It was a few days before the christening of the Crown Princess. The King and Queen's firstborn, Princess Sativa, was to have the biggest celebration. Guests came from all over the kingdom, and further, too. My brothers thought Christmas had come early, there were so many carriages to rob. And they made the mistake of robbing the Princess's godmother."

Brogan looked puzzled. Remembering her brothers' confusion, Alba decided to explain.

"The Princess is unusual in that she has a fairy godmother, a powerful enchantress who watches over her. A witch, if you will. My brothers had me run up to the carriage, in a fair panic, to beg for their help. When everyone was distracted, my brothers took what they wanted. I ran up, and a lady climbed out. She swore she would help me, and for a moment, I believed her, but then I could hear shouts from behind her and my brothers came flying out of the carriage to land on the ground beside me, their arms full of her jewels and things. She made my brothers really small, telling them how they could only break the curse with hard work and charity, but they howled over her about how I had helped them, that all they did was for me, and how I was just as deserving of punishment as they were. She turned to me, looking really disappointed, I remember, and said, 'So must it be,' before she cursed me, too. The next thing I knew, we were in the cellar here, and my brothers made it their mission to make sure no one ever lived here long enough to make them do a day's work."

"Unlike you." Brogan's voice cut through her dark thoughts.

"Oh, this is hardly work," Alba said. "I love painting. I always have. If I could choose anything to do in life, it would be this. There's something about creating something beautiful from nothing. And, when it's done, making something else. No two the same, ever, because I am not the same. Some days I am happy, or sad, or reflective, or angry at my brothers, or hungry and wishing I had a jam-cake." She smiled to soften what sounded like an accusation. "I know why there are none tonight, of course. But other nights, my brothers sometimes stole it before I could come up here."

This got Brogan's attention. "Come up here? You mean you live here with me?"

"We sleep in the secret cupboard in the cellar. All the houses hereabouts have them. Most of them use it to hold a still for liquor or perhaps a strongbox, but yours has been a house for elves." A sudden thought occurred to her. "Where do you keep your strongbox? If my brothers know, they would have tried to take it with them when they left."

Brogan turned pale. "I heard clinking sounds last night and didn't think…" He raced up the ladder to the loft, then came down, shaking his head. "It's gone. All of it."

Alba cursed her brothers, then cursed them again. "They will pay for what they've done to you," she swore.

"And to you. What they've done to both of us, and who knows how many others? There will be justice," Brogan said.

Alba stared at him for a moment. He truly meant what he said. "There shall," she said.

Thirty-Five

Darkness gathered, on the night before Christmas. Brogan hoped against hope for a knock that he had not yet heard when someone tapped tentatively at his door.

"We're closed!" he called. "No more shoes until the new year!" He set down the pair he'd been making, the tiniest, most delicate boots he'd ever beheld. Even then, he suspected they'd be too big for Alba, but he couldn't trust these to anyone else.

"It's for your niece, sir," came Drogo's voice.

Brogan threw open the door and embraced the startled boy. He traded the package for a purse of silver, wished the boy a good Christmas, and shut the door again.

Brogan untied the package of clothing with feverish hands. They had to be perfect. Nothing less would do for Alba. He breathed a sigh of relief when the contents of the parcel met with his approval. He took a moment to buff the boots before adding them to the parcel and tying it up again. He hid the bundle under a pile of leather, hoping Alba wouldn't find it.

Tonight, he would give her the clothes she'd asked for and she'd be free.

Free of the curse.

Free to go and live whatever life she chose.

Far from him.

Brogan's heart froze in his chest. She would leave, just like her brothers had, and he'd never see her again.

Clothes and boots would not be enough. Alba deserved everything, and if that's what she wanted, then she would have it.

Brogan seized his cloak and threw it around

his shoulders. He needed one more thing before Christmas, and if he had to break down the door to get it, he would.

Thirty-Six

Alba's first Christmas Eve without her family felt strange. Not that her brothers had ever bought her gifts, though her father always had. She'd considered making a gift for Brogan, but it didn't seem right to take his leather and paint, only to give them back to him disguised as a gift. Oh, she could craft him a pretty pair of boots, but his own were so fine, it would be silly to attempt to replace them with her own ordinary work. He was no fine lady, to want painted dancing slippers.

The other shops in the street had shut early,

much like Brogan had done here, so that they might enjoy a dinner with their family before the cathedral bells summoned them to the midnight mass that marked the start of the Christmas period.

She hadn't attended such a mass in years, and the ones in her memory held a kind of magic. Thousands of candles, reflected by the snow outside and the shiny mosaics inside. The whole city awake and celebrating at a time when they were normally asleep. Despite Brogan's promises, she couldn't quite make herself believe that tonight she might finally join them once more.

After all, he'd forgotten about her, hadn't he? He'd left at dusk, heading out in a rush, perhaps late to dinner with his family. He had a brother who was married, a shoemaker on the other side of town. She'd heard him talk about gifts for his niece and nephews when he sent Drogo out on errands, so the couple evidently had children, too. Christmas was a time for family, so of course he would spend as much time as possible with them.

She had run out of shoes to paint. The last

orders had gone earlier in the day, Christmas shoes covered in mistletoe vines. Brogan had even sent Drogo out to find her some mistletoe that she might use as a model to paint the design. The bunch had sat on the table beside her since yesterday, but she'd hung it from the rafters to dry now the shoes were all done.

Perhaps she should make a start on the orders for the new year – that could be her gift to Brogan. Less that he would have to do later. And it would be nice to make shoes again. She'd spent so much time painting, she'd barely sewn a stitch. She didn't want to lose her skills, for they were the only thing she had.

Yet for a moment, she dreamed what it might be like if Brogan had brought her clothes, like he'd done for her brothers. She would be free to join the rest of the city at the midnight mass, and afterward…

Afterward, she would have no home to go to. She would have to take sanctuary at the cathedral, or find a convent willing to take her in. For she had nothing. She was nothing.

At least here she was warm, and dry, and

could make pretty shoes.

Everything she'd ever wanted was here, within these four walls. Why would she ever want to leave?

It was for the best that Brogan had forgotten to bring her clothes, Alba told herself. Freedom was a fine thing for some, but she wouldn't know what to do with it.

Thirty-Seven

A gust of wind caught Brogan's cloak as he opened the door, and he found himself doing a silly sort of twirl to get free of it before he could close the door behind him, shutting out the cold.

"The old men say it will snow before morning," he said.

Alba smiled and set down her sewing. "That will be pretty to see."

Would she still be here in the morning? Or ever? Brogan's mouth was terribly dry. The house would be empty without her, and so would his heart.

"I asked Drogo to bring us dinner. I left it by the fire so it would stay warm," he said, rushing to the hearth. He set out their meal, keeping his gaze firmly on the table so he wouldn't meet her eyes. Was it wrong to want one last meal with her before she left him forever?

Yes, he owed her the freedom he'd promised, and he would give her everything she'd asked for before the night was over.

He just wanted one more night, was all. One night with her to remember after she'd left.

For no amount of gold would be enough, he knew. Not for a girl who could mint the stuff with a paintbrush. She could present herself at court to the Queen, and claim her place as Royal Shoemaker, just like her father once had. She didn't need him at all.

"I thought you would share a meal with your brother and his family," Alba said.

Brogan laughed. "His wife will have none of me at the moment. She's with child, and it makes her terribly ill. My brother has asked me to stay away until the babe is born. He has wanted children for so long, he would do almost anything to keep it safe."

"As a good father should." The words came out sounding so bleak, Brogan found himself staring at her.

But her father had left her in the care of her brothers, and her brothers had…

Deserted her. Brogan would never do that.

He bowed deeply. "I am new to being a host, for this is my first Yule here, but I hope this small feast is good enough for you, Alba."

"Venison stew, dumplings…and cake. This is hardly a small feast."

No, that it was not. Brogan sat down, and she shifted along the bench until she sat across from him. There was silence as they ate, until Brogan realised he'd forgotten something.

"The wine!" he cried, shoving his bench back from the table.

Her stew slopped out of her bowl and splattered across her front. Alba swabbed at it ineffectually with a cloth, but she only spread the stuff further. "Times like these, I wish I had something else to wear." She rose from the table. "Please excuse me. I must go wash."

Brogan swallowed. It was time. Now, or never.

"Please. Take these with you," he said, pulled the wrapped bundle from under the pile of leather.

"Brogan…" She sounded so uncertain. Tears glistened in her eyes.

He bowed his head. "I keep my promises."

Thirty-Eight

Alba drew a bucket of water from the water butt and hid in the shadow of the cask, where Brogan wouldn't see her undress. The once-stiff sack had worn so thin in places it was as soft as linen, but the coarse weave had left stew on her skin. Alba washed herself, then dunked the sack in the bucket, scrubbing at the stain until it was back to its normal shade of brown. She wrung most of the moisture from it, but it would still be some time before it dried in front of the fire.

That left the bundle Brogan had given her.

With shaking hands, she untied the thongs holding the leather covering together. It was softer than the stuff she made shoes with – this would make beautiful gloves, she thought.

Then the wrapping parted, and her mouth dropped open. A bundle of blue and white wool nestled in the leather, like a gift from heaven itself. A creamy underdress in wool so soft it must have come from a lamb. Another in linen, so finely woven she could see through it. Blushing a little, Alba reached for the blue. This gown was far from transparent – it was made of thick, felted wool, warm enough to keep out the cold even on a winter's night, though it was the colour of the ultramarine night sky. And beneath it…a gown that was surely silk, as bright as the sky in summer.

Alba wanted to cry. She could never wear something so beautiful – she was a shoemaker's daughter, not a court lady.

But if she was to wear a wet sack or warm wool, Alba would make her choice. She wouldn't want to appear ungrateful for Brogan's generous gift.

She slipped on the underdress, and the

matching hose. The blue woollen overdress laced up the front, letting a little of the underdress show through. She longed to see herself, but there were no mirrors in Brogan's shop. Something she should suggest to him, for his feminine clients would certainly like to see themselves wearing their new purchases.

"Does it fit?" Brogan asked.

Like the gloves that would one day be made from the leather wrapping, Alba thought. "Yes," she said.

"Even the boots? I thought I might have made them too big."

Boots? Alba lifted up the precious silk dress, and found there was more. A cloak with deep blue felt on the outside, lined with lambs' wool, and beneath that…a pair of Brogan's finely crafted boots. She didn't need more than a glance to know they were precisely her size.

He had done this for her. All for her.

Alba slumped onto a stool, rocking a little as she tried to blink back her tears before they could fall. No one had ever been this kind to her. No one. She didn't deserve this. She didn't…

"May I help you with the boots? I can remake them if they are not right," Brogan said, peering over the water butt.

Unable to speak, Alba nodded.

His warm hand enveloped her foot, his touch unmistakeable even through her stockings. With great care, he eased her foot into the boot and set it on the floor.

One more boot, and she would lose her home again – perhaps for the last time.

She burst into tears.

"What's wrong? Does it hurt? Did I make it too small?" Brogan asked, tearing the boot off her foot so he could examine it.

"No, it fits perfectly," she whispered, not willing to lie to him.

He stared at the boot for a long moment, before he let it fall to the floor. "But it is not good enough. I saw that you had clothes suitable for court, but even the unadorned shoes you make are far finer than these. Boots fit for commoners, that's all I am fit to make. Whereas you…you deserve something finer. Shoes fit for a queen. I will begin again."

Alba opened her mouth to protest that she

was as highborn as he, with no aspirations to wear court shoes, ever. All she wanted to do was make them.

But if she did, she'd have to put on his gift, and her days as a shoemaker would be over.

His gift – shoes and all – were more than she deserved.

"No, give them to me. I shall put them on. They are perfect," she choked out, holding out her hands for the boots.

But he refused to give them to her. "They are far from it, I'm afraid. I should not have given them to you in such a state, but it's Christmas Eve, and I wanted to thank you properly. In my impatience, I make a poor shoemaker indeed. Please forget you ever saw boots such as these, and allow me to make you something more suitable."

Gratefully, she acceded.

He took her hands and kissed them. "Thank you."

Her skin tingled at his touch, and she felt her face grow hot. Ducking her head to hide her blush, Alba mumbled, "I'd best go see if my things are dry yet. It would be a terrible crime should I spill paint on something as beautiful as this gown."

Within moments, normalcy was restored, as she smoothed the softened sacking against her skin before sitting at the worktable. If her heart beat a little faster in her breast, she did her best to ignore it.

Thirty-Nine

She barely noticed when Brogan bade her farewell to go to the Christmas mass in the cathedral. She had not attended church since her father's funeral – her brothers were as faithless about their faith as most other aspects of their lives.

She wondered at the state of her soul, that she was not willing to don the boots Brogan had given her so that she might attend mass. Even if she had, she suspected no amount of religious fervour would be enough to atone for getting cursed in the first place. Or for choosing to remain cursed, rather than go to church.

Alba shook her head. Let the priests worry about the state of her soul, should she have a chance to meet one again. She was a shoemaker, not some scholar, and it was best that she occupy her worried mind with working leather.

Brogan might have chosen to take a week's holiday, but he had orders enough for the new year to keep her busy day and night until year's end.

She unrolled a piece of leather on the worktable, and set to work.

She had begun to cut out the third pair of shoes when the door slammed open, sending a vanguard of icy air to assault the warmth of her safe haven.

If cold air was to be her only unwelcome visitor, Alba would have closed the door, and forgotten all about it. However, her two brothers, each easily thrice her size, crowded in, making her wish that perhaps she had gone to mass with Brogan and the other townsfolk.

Alba's heart fluttered within her chest as she

backed away. "What – what are you doing here?" she asked, her voice trembling as though it had taken a chill from the air coming through the still open door.

Onni kicked the door shut behind him and grunted.

Gad looked her up and down. "Why are you still small? The curse is broken."

Alba shook her head. "For you, maybe. Not for me. He gave you clothes, but not me." She hoped her face did not betray her lie. She swallowed. "You should go. He knows you took his money. If he finds you here, he will summon the guards and –"

Onni seized her arm. "We're not leaving without you," he said. "You're our family. There is no way we'll let some stranger profit from your labour."

Alba's heart softened. Perhaps her brothers did care for her after all.

"The whorehouse won't take a girl so small, the madam said," Gad said. He frowned. "But we can't leave you here, either. That bastard's getting your services for free."

Alba's heart died a little more. She might

not be certain of her soul, but her brothers were both damned. "It is my life, and my services," she hissed with vehemence. "I choose whether I make shoes or lie on my back or pretend to be in need of assistance while you rob my benefactors blind. Not you."

Gad backhanded her with his free hand. "Tell that to the madam who buys you, and she'll have you whipped. And she will buy you, mark my words. There are plenty of men who like their girls young, and unbroken. Especially ones as pretty as you." He yanked her arm, pulling her toward the door.

Alba planted her feet. "I will not!"

But it was no good. Onni picked her up bodily from behind, and no amount of kicking or screaming would make him let go.

Gad grabbed a sack, emptied the contents unceremoniously on the floor, and with Onni's help, shoved her inside, head first. One of them must have tied the sack shut, and, judging from the smell, shoved the sack under his coat. She could scarcely breathe, but she forced herself to drag in a lung full of foul-smelling air so that she might scream loud enough for someone to hear her and help.

Muffled by the sack and her brother's clothes, she could hear their worried voices, but not the words. But no amount of cloth could protect her from the bite of the icy wind as her brothers opened the door.

But the wind carried more than cold this time. Alba thought she could hear the strains of a song, and the shrill cry of a baby. Was the mass over, with people returning to their homes? She hoped so. If she could hear them, they would definitely hear her.

She screamed, then sucked in a breath and screamed again. Her brother drew the sack out from under his coat and slammed it against the wall, knocking the breath from her lungs and all thoughts from her head, if only for a moment. The sack, with her inside, tumbled to the floor, as though her brothers felt one blow was not punishment enough.

"Brutes! You're both uncaring, unfeeling brutes! Lazy, useless —"

"Alba? Is that you?" This voice belonged to Brogan, not either of her brothers.

Someone fumbled with the mouth of the

sack, unfastening it so that Alba could climb out. She found herself sitting in a puddle of coarse cloth, on the threshold of Brogan's open door. She tried to take a step out, to see where her brothers had gone, but she smacked into an invisible barrier, as though the open door were closed to her. Was that the wall the sack had hit, tumbling down it to deposit her on the floor? Had this cursed barrier saved her from her brothers?

"What happened?" Brogan asked.

Alba drew in a deep breath, then another. Even a third was not enough to still the shakiness in her tone as she said, "My brothers were here. They tried to take me…take me to sell me." As a whore, her treacherous mind added, but she could not bring herself to say the words. For Brogan to think of her so…she could not bear it. Better to be cursed than what her brothers wanted her for.

The curse had saved her from a terrible fate.

So she had been right to refuse to put on the shoes, she reflected. For surely worse damnation waited for her in whatever hell her brothers had in mind for her.

Forty

The summer sun shone on Penelope's bare feet as she dangled them over the canal. The enchanted horse lurked beneath the surface, ready to be buried and forgotten when the canal was filled in on the morrow.

She reached for another peach. The trees had been moved to another island, and where they had once grown was now covered in cobblestones, set in such a way that they looked like fish scales. Soon, the whole campo, including the canal beneath her feet, would be payed over to become Saint Mark's Square, where two emperors, a Northman king, the Pope, and her father would sign the peace treaties that divided the world between them. Three princes and three princesses would be married, and the hostilities would be over.

They would all stay to witness the annual ceremony where the Duke walked out to the edge of the sandbank protecting the city and said the city's marriage vows to the sea. This year, the Pope had not only agreed to officiate, but he'd given the Duke a gold ring to throw into the water to signify how he blessed the union.

It seemed almost an anticlimax to have weddings instead of a big battle, but that's how things were done in the Republic of Rialto.

"What do you want to do next?" Godfrey asked Penelope.

She threw her peach stone into the canal. "Hope there is something cool to drink in the kitchen. It used to be lovely here under the trees, but now the sun beats down on you unmercifully."

He chuckled. "I mean after the treaties are signed. Would you like to live here, or come home with me, where we can ride every day, or did you have some other adventure in mind?"

Penelope considered. "I would like to spend the rest of the summer somewhere cooler. And there's my dowry…My brothers used it to finance a shipping expedition to the northern seas, but the ship and cargo were taken by pirates, after reaching Beacon Isle. Once the treaty is signed, we could find a ship headed to northern waters, and see if we can find my dowry…along with the rest of the pirate treasure."

Godfrey laughed, then realised she hadn't joined him. "You mean you are serious?"

Penelope shrugged. "It's a sizeable sum. Well worth tracking down, so that any children we have might have the money to join my family business in Rialto, if that is their wish, or buy more breeding stock for your horse herds." She smiled. "More importantly, it is another adventure, where we will not have to worry about saving one another. Just…enjoy things as they happen. Will you take me on an adventure, Sir Godfrey? Just a knight and his lady, no one else?"

He could not refuse her anything, and she knew it. "If you want an adventure, my lovely lady wife, then you shall have one. I hear the pirates around Beacon Isle are quite lovely this time of year."

Forty-One

In the coming days, Brogan was true to his word – or as true as an oathbreaker could be. Both a bar and a bolt were fitted to the door, which were to be fastened whenever he left the house, or when one of them slept.

He had a second bed placed in the loft, ostensibly for an apprentice that he had not yet hired. He found it hard not to choke on the thought of Alba ever being his apprentice when her skill surpassed his in so many ways, but the lie was easier for others to accept than the truth.

Unable to bear seeing Alba still wearing a sack when she should have been wearing clothing of much better quality, he sent Drogo back to the same tailor, with an order for some workday dresses and underclothes. He knew little of the lives of fine ladies, but he knew that in rich houses both the stillroom and the brewhouse were places where the castle chatelaine might reside. Such a lady would surely wish to train her daughter in the same skills, for she might be mistress of a fine household, too, one day. Brogan almost choked again at the thought of Alba or any niece of his as mistress of a fine castle, but Drogo didn't seem to notice. Like the clever boy he was, he ran off to carry out his errand with all of his usual eagerness and efficiency.

When her new clothing was delivered, Alba almost refused to wear any of it, saying it was still too fine for the likes of her. But when she found an apron, made of thick, dark linen that would protect her clothing from neck to ankle, she relented. Brogan did not dare tell her that the aprons were made to the same pattern as those worn by the Crown Princess.

The first time he saw Alba wearing her workday wool, he was reminded anew of his oath to protect her. New clothing might protect her modesty, but it would not be enough against her brothers.

At the end of the day, when he sent Drogo home, he followed the boy out into the street, where Alba could not go. Once out of her hearing, he told Drogo, "I want you to keep a watch. You – and all your young friends, those who are too young to be apprenticed yet. One of you is to watch my house at all times, when I am home and especially when I am not. Should any of you hear a woman scream –"

"Like the girl ghost at Christmas Eve?" Drogo interrupted excitedly.

Brogan frowned. He wished he could tell the boy the truth, but who would believe him? At least the boy believed in ghosts. "Perhaps, though it might not be as loud as that. The sound of a woman in distress, or of a struggle inside my house –"

"Is it true that ghosts can do that? Throw things? My friend Peter said –"

"Yes." Brogan took a deep breath. He

prayed Alba could not hear him. "If you hear the ghost doing any of those things inside my house, have someone send for the city guards. They will know what to do."

Drogo's eyes widened. "The guards can fight ghosts? I thought only priests could do that!" He looked particularly impressed.

"They will know what to do," Brogan repeated. "Will you see that a watch is kept?"

Drogo nodded and raced off.

Brogan's shoulders slumped. What more could he do? He was not some lord who could employ a squad of knights to guard his door. Drogo and the other street urchins would have to do.

He prayed it would be enough.

Forty-Two

With most of his customers expecting the shop to be closed until the new year, the newly installed bell rang rarely that week. Yet on New Year's Eve, Brogan was surprised to hear a decisive tug on the bell. When he did not answer the door immediately, a second, more forceful tug followed the first.

Brogan hurried to unbolt the door. He found himself facing a grey-haired woman with a determined expression on her face. "How may I help you, mistress?" he asked.

Her clothes were of good quality, though

her fur-lined cloak looked worn beneath its light dusting of snow. Perhaps she was the wife of some wealthy merchant, for everything about her clothes spoke of practicality, not the spectacle of court.

The woman pursed her lips. "I have come for some new shoes for my goddaughter," she said. "It seems she has outgrown all hers, but she will not wear anything that has not been painted." She glanced down at her own feet. Despite the snow caking them, her boots looked as well worn as any of Brogan's. "And it seems I may need a new pair as well."

"We have been very busy with orders for court," Brogan said smoothly, spreading his hands wide. "But if you allow me to take your measurements and those of your daughter, perhaps I might find time between now and February –"

The sound of Alba swearing was enough to make him forget whatever he might have wanted to say.

"Please excuse me," he said to the old woman and closed the door in her face.

He turned to face Alba, her eyes wide and

scared as though she seen a ghost. "Tell her she shall have her shoes tomorrow," Alba hissed. "She is the witch who cast the curse, and if she sees me…"

A flash of ruddy light sparked near the fire, growing larger and larger until the flaming circle almost reached the ceiling. The witch stepped through her portal, before the flames vanished.

"It's not wise to anger a witch," the woman said, lowering her hood and shaking snow from her cloak. "Or to make them wait. As those who have already done so can tell you."

Alba quailed beneath the witch's gaze. Yet when she spoke, her voice was anything but weak. "I will make whatever shoes you wish, working day and night until they are done. But only if you do no harm to Brogan here, and do not darken his door again. Your curse has done enough that he did not deserve."

The witch's eyes narrowed. She removed her cloak, and hung it on the hook by the door. Next, she helped herself to a cup of the mulled wine sitting in a jug on the hearth. Finally, she seated herself on the bench where

Brogan usually measured his clients' feet. She took a sip from her wine cup, then said, "I felt the curse break. Yet here you stand, as if it had not. The court swirls with stories of a shoemaker of such skill that he must surely have sold his soul to the devil, yet I recognise the work, work that was not done by his hand at all." She fixed her gaze on Alba once again. "On the day we met, you tried to spin me a story of how you needed my help, and I recall a promise that was made. Yet the story changed, when your family appeared and I had neither the time nor the patience to hear it. So I cast a curse, meaning to come back, to see if you had learned your lesson. Yet now…it seems you still have a story to tell. Now I have a seat by the fire, with a full cup in my hand, I believe it is time that I heard it."

Brogan opened his mouth, not sure where to start.

Alba got in first. "I will tell it," she said, "but I must ask Brogan to send for some more mulled wine, because my tale is a long one."

Forty-Three

Drogo had gone home for dinner, and it would be faster for Brogan to head to the tavern himself than to bother the boy, so Alba waited for Brogan to leave before she settled on the stool beside the witch's chair.

"How many times did you accost carriages on their way to the city, to beg for their help?" the witch asked.

"I do not know," Alba said frankly. "My brothers kept telling me that this would be the last, but it never was, and by the time I realised it, it was too late to count. Yet I had no choice

– if I did not do as they asked, they would beat me, starve me, or threaten to sell me. So I did as they commanded. Preying upon the kind-hearted women who rode in carriages. While my brothers slipped inside and stole things, those fine ladies tried to help me. Of course, it wasn't always women. There were rich men, too, too fat to ride a horse, or too lazy." Alba swallowed. "The sort of men who see a maiden in distress as a gift from the heavens to amuse them on their journey." Tears welled up, but she blinked them back. No wonder her brothers wanted to sell her to a whorehouse – she had not been a maiden for a very long time.

"How many men?"

Alba glared at the witch. "What does it matter? One was too many – more than any girl should have forced upon her."

"And the handsome young shoemaker, too?"

Alba rose to her full height. "Leave Brogan out of this. He is a good man – a rare thing in this city – who has not laid a hand on me except to help me up."

"So he has not made a deal with the devil?"

Alba snorted. "Of course not, unless that devil is me. Cursed into a creature many might call a kind of devil. By you."

"What kind of deal? You make him the greatest shoemaker in the land…and what? He will break the curse?"

"My brothers tried to destroy his shop. They broke his tools, burned what they could, and destroyed what was left. I only meant to make a pair of shoes, a small gift to replace what was taken, but…" Alba shook her head. "I could not have known they could create such fervour at court." Or that she could not resist the call to work with leather again.

"No one has seen such shoes since the Crown Princess's christening. Your father's work was always exquisite, and you have inherited his gift."

"I made the shoes for the Princess," Alba said. "My father's hands were none too steady toward the end, and such delicate work fell to me long before that. I suspect my mother did most of it, too, until she died."

The witch considered this for a long

moment, before she said, "So you agreed to bring the shoemaker fame and fortune, in exchange for what?"

Alba shook her head again. "I promised him nothing. I merely made shoes, as I always have, except when I was stuck here with my brothers and no one would rent the shop. That is all I have ever wanted. If my father had lived longer, or if my brothers had been willing to learn his trade, as I was, I would still be here."

"He will never let you go, you know. He cannot, not if he wants to keep selling shoes to the court." There was pity in the witch's eyes.

Alba did not want this woman's pity. Not now she was happy.

"Why would I want him to let me go? He gave me clothes far finer than the ones he had made for my brothers. He even made boots that would fit my feet – perhaps the finest pair he has ever made. He has sworn more than once he will set me free, and he has kept his word. All I need to do to break the curse you cast upon me is to dress in silk and soft leather –"

"So why don't you?"

"Because if I do, there is nothing holding me here. My brothers will have me back in an instant, ripping the fine clothes into rags, throwing me in front of carriages until they tire of banditry, when they will sell me as a whore for enough coin to fill their bellies. I would rather live the rest of my life naked and cursed, here in this house, where I might do the one thing I love most, than to leave." Alba's eyes flashed. "You promised to help me, and I say you have kept your promise. I have my work, the one thing I wished for most. Now leave me to it, and leave Brogan alone, too. Your conscience is clear. Begone, witch."

The witch did not move, merely looking thoughtful. "Dalia. Mistress Dalia, to those who recognise the rarity of an enchantress or want a favour from one, but Dalia will do. Especially as it seems I already owe you a favour, and likely a second for what I must ask you to do."

Alba opened her mouth to utter a decisive NO.

"Oh, I know you wish to refuse, but wait until you hear what I have to offer. Even you cannot refuse this, surely. For what I must ask you could keep your brothers from ever bothering you again."

It was as though the witch could read her mind. Perhaps she could. Alba pressed her lips together and gave a tiny nod to indicate the witch might continue.

"There is a sort of law among those with magical blood. We do not betray those we pledge our loyalty to, and while we are permitted to use our magic in ways that might harm others, we are only supposed to curse those who truly deserve it. It is customary to create a key to breaking a curse, too, so that if the punished should ever repent, they might be freed from a curse they no longer deserve."

"I don't want – " Alba began.

"Ah, but this isn't about you. This is about your brothers, who have robbed you as surely as any of their other victims, for they stole freedom that they did not earn. It isn't your fault, but mine – a mistake I must correct. Your brothers must be caught, and punished properly for their crimes. And as I have failed to do this the first time, I must ask for your help in accomplishing my task on my second try." The witch met Alba's gaze and held it. "In return, I offer you anything that is within my power to grant, magical or otherwise. A wish, if you will. Two, if you are truly innocent of your brothers' crimes. What do you say? Will you help me?"

"I will," Brogan said grimly as he shouldered open the door. "They burned my shop, stole and destroyed my supplies, then ran off with what rightfully belonged to Alba. I will help you, but not for wishes." He turned his burning gaze on Alba. "My price is that you will do everything in your power to see that Alba is safe. That her brothers cannot harm her again."

The witch gave a nod. "Then we have the same goal."

This seemed to satisfy Brogan, who began to set their dinner upon the table.

But Alba was far from satisfied. She knew witches, and this one in particular, were twisty in their dealings. Her mother had told her many tales about what happened to those who broke a bargain made with a witch, and none of them had ended well. Not that she thought Brogan would break any bargain he made – he was too honest for that.

So honest he might believe they had a bargain before the witch had agreed to one…a witch who might turn on him at any time, for nothing truly bound her to him, or his cause.

But the witch had offered Alba wishes in exchange for her help. If Alba agreed, then the witch truly would be her ally, and bound to help Brogan, too.

"I will help you," Alba said slowly, "in exchange for what you have promised."

Now the witch's eyes were on her, too. "We have a deal, then."

Alba should have felt relieved, but the cold hand of fate slipped around her heart, making her shiver instead.

Forty-Four

Sunday dawned, and with it Alba's deepening dread. The virtuous had all gone to church, leaving her alone in Brogan's house. If the witch, Dalia, was right, then her brothers would appear, and she could lay the trap they had planned.

Alba half wanted Dalia to be wrong, but the neighbours' voices had no sooner died away before she heard the sound she dreaded.

"Knock, knock, little sister!"

She wanted to run, to hide, to do anything but answer the door and allow Onni and Gad inside, but she had made a deal with a witch, and she would not be the one to break it.

Instead, she forced herself to stand her ground as her brothers entered the house.

Onni dumped a bundle of rags on the table. "Put these on. Clothes are what breaks the curse."

Alba eyed the bundle. She preferred her sack. "Those are rags, not clothes. Whatever happened to robbing the rich in their carriages on the road? Surely they'd be wearing silk and stuff like that."

Gad spat on the floor. "Carriages can't make it through the snow, silly girl. Won't be any more of those until spring."

For the first time in his life, Gad had given her a gift: the perfect opening. "That's not what I heard," Alba said slowly. "I heard they keep the road open to the mines south east of the city. There's so much salt there, they use it to melt the snow for their supply carts. Salt comes to the city for the King's cellars, and he sends gold and supplies back. Every week."

Onni stared at her. "Where'd you hear that?"

"I listen to the customers, when they come

in here to be measured up for new shoes. Lots of court folk come here, and they like to talk. I heard the supply wagon broke a wheel this week, so it'll have twice the gold when it goes next week." She forced out a laugh. "Half the salt ended up in the snow, so the less important courtiers didn't get any salt on their feasting tables this week. Some of Brogan's customers were most upset. And the week before that – "

Gad waved her into silence. "I don't want to hear the common gossip about town. Useless women's prattle."

Onni looked thoughtful. He leaned over to whisper something in Gad's ear. Gad looked suspicious at first, but then he slowly nodded.

"You keep those clothes somewhere safe. We'll come back for you," Onni said, tugging on Gad's arm.

"Don't you even think of running away!" Gad added, shaking a finger as he headed out the door.

"Where would I go?" Alba called after them, but they were already outside in the street by then, so she doubted they'd heard. She crossed the room and pulled the door shut, praying to anyone who'd listen that her brothers would take the bait and attack the cart.

When they did…Dalia and Brogan would be waiting. With a whole troop of guards to arrest them, she hoped.

Forty-Five

Alba reached for a cloth to wet the leather, so that she could stamp a design into the new shoe. But her fingers closed over the lip of the bucket without touching cloth – the benighted cloth had fallen in again. Swearing, she climbed onto the table to peer into the bucket. Something she wouldn't have to do if she was normal-sized, a nagging voice in the back of her mind reminded her.

Yes, things had been much easier before the curse, before her father had died, when she'd been an ordinary shoemaker's apprentice who hoped her work might please the King and earn her the title of Royal Shoemaker and a shop of her own one day. But she'd take this over the alternative any day.

Of course, the cloth sat in the bottom of the bucket, taunting her. Alba reached in. Her fingertips burned as she touched ice, and she let out a little shriek. By all that was holy, the stuff was cold.

"Are you well?" Brogan asked sleepily from the loft above. He'd retired for the night – as most people would, for the church bells had chimed midnight not long since – but Alba had wanted to work on.

"Fine," she replied through gritted teeth as she thrust her whole arm into the bucket, leaning over the side so that she could reach the bottom. Damn, it was cold. So cold she could scarcely feel her fingers, or the cloth she should be touching by now. One…more…inch…

She stretched up onto her toes, setting all her weight on the side of the bucket as her feet lost contact with the table altogether, and still it was not enough. Just a little further…

Too much.

She slipped, the bucket sloshed, and in a heartbeat she tumbled from the table, a second shriek tearing loose from her lips that turned into a full-throated scream as the freezing water drenched her on the way down.

Then darkness descended.

Forty-Six

Brogan was already out of bed and on his way to the ladder when a shriek, a clatter, followed by a heartrending scream had him leaping from the loft, landing in a crouch, the ladder forgotten.

"Alba?" he asked uncertainly.

Her seat sat empty, though her tools still waited to be put to use in decorating the plain-looking shoes beside them.

His eyed darted to the door, but it was barred, as always at this time of night. Her brothers could not have come in and taken her.

"Alba? Are you all right?"

He approached the table. Ice cold water seeped through his socks to bite at his toes, before he realised the floor was awash.

The bucket that had held all the water now lay on its side, partially obscuring the motionless figure behind it.

Alba.

She lay in the deepest part of the puddle, soaked to the skin. He gathered her in his arms, desperate to make sure she was still breathing. If her chest moved, he couldn't see it beneath the apron she wore to protect her clothes. He held a hand to her lips, praying that he hadn't lost her. The warmth of her breath against his palm almost drove him to tears.

She lived.

But he had to get her out of her wet things and into something warm, lest she fall ill. That's where he balked, for though she felt like little more than a child in his arms, he knew she was a woman grown. A woman who would not thank him for undressing her.

He found a blanket and wrapped her in that, not willing to let her go.

"Alba, please wake. I am…I don't know what to do."

If he lost her, he, too, would be lost.

He should have made her better boots, so the curse would already be broken, and a bucket would not have nearly crushed her.

"Ow." Alba's eyes blinked open.

He couldn't help it. He kissed her.

Forty-Seven

Alba's head hurt, making her wish she could retreat into oblivion once more, but someone held her, sending alarm bells tolling in her already ringing head. Her brothers…they couldn't be…

She opened her eyes to Brogan's worried face, before the creases of worry were wiped away by surprise and blissful relief.

Hers as well as his, for he meant her no harm.

Then his lips captured hers, shocking her breathless.

Warm and tentative, yet for all his gentleness, his lips stamped their mark on her as readily as she marked every shoe she made. She parted her lips to draw breath, and the breath was as much his as hers, a shared gasp at such a surprising, yet natural moment.

She'd never shared a kiss with a lover before – never had a lover, for the brutish pawings of the noblemen who'd ravished her had quenched any lustful feelings she might have had – but this…Brogan's lips on hers, melting her so completely both inside and out…

She wanted to take him to bed now, so that some mutual ravishing might take place. The sort where she could remove her wet clothes and he could…

A mighty hammering came from the door.

"Brogan the shoemaker, open this door in the name of the King! If we find the woman with you has come to harm, then you will be spending the rest of the night in the castle dungeons!" The guard bellowed so loud, it hurt to hear him. He would wake half the city if Brogan didn't open the door.

Brogan's panicked eyes met hers. "Hide!" he

hissed, setting her on her feet.

Yes. Alba held onto Brogan for a moment, to make sure she could stand, before she clambered up the ladder, as fast as she could. From the loft, she headed for her favourite hiding place among the rafters, where she was small enough to see from the shadows without being seen.

Two guardsmen barged into the house, their armour making Brogan seem small in comparison.

"Your neighbours reported a woman screaming in distress inside your house. Where is she?" one guard demanded.

Brogan shrugged. "You may search the place from top to bottom, but you'll find no one here but me."

"Who screamed, then?" the other guard asked.

Another shrug. "Perhaps one of the neighbours. A nightmare, or someone falling out of bed. Maybe they saw a spider in the outhouse. Or maybe – "

The first guard held up his hand for silence. "No. The boy said the scream came from here.

From the shoemaker's house."

Brogan's shoulders sagged for a moment before he regained his composure. "It must have been the ghost, then. This house is haunted. Ask anyone, for it's common knowledge."

The first guard turned to the second. "Search the house. I'll see that he doesn't interfere."

The second guard nodded, then headed for the steps to the cellar.

Brogan raised his hands in open surrender. "I have no intention of interfering. Please search the house. If you find the ghost, tell her not to wake the neighbours next time."

The first guard frowned. "Does your ghost scream often?"

Brogan forced out a laugh. "Perhaps. I confess I tend to ignore it now, particularly when I'm working." He waved his hand at the worktable, where Alba's tools still sat, with the shoes she'd planned to finish tonight. The water had missed the table and mostly ended up on the floor, to her relief. Two pairs of finished shoes, their paint still wet, lined up on a bench before the fire, warming their toes.

The first guard headed for the bench and reached for a shoe.

"Don't touch those!" Brogan shouted, leaping to block the guard. "Those are a commission for the Keeper of the Treasury's wife. Her daughter is to be presented to the Queen next week as one of her new ladies in waiting, and she was very particular about the design. The flower is a family emblem, and the pigments came from the Holy Land, at great cost. Those shoes are worth more than you make in a year."

Actually, the white flowers were painted with lime, one of the cheaper pigments Brogan bought from the tanner when he ordered another load of leather. Now, the blue she used for the night sky came from the markets at the Holy Land, and the price was as astronomical as the stars she painted upon it, but courtiers craved that blue so much, they were willing to pay almost anything to see it on their shoes. So Brogan charged them accordingly, and bought her more blue.

The guard didn't seem to notice Brogan's

lie. Instead, he shouted down to his colleague, "Hey, Moimir! Don't ever bring Jarka here. This man makes shoes for the quality. All painted like the artwork in the cathedral. You should see them!"

Moimir came up the cellar steps, shaking his head. "Only a fool would want paintings on shoes. Like you, Dmitriy. And the only people who'd buy such a thing are those with more money than sense." He sighed. "No women in the cellar. I'm beginning to believe it might be a ghost. Better check the loft to be sure, though." He headed up the ladder.

"Do you have a woman in the house?" Dmitriy asked Brogan.

"If I did, she'd be making me supper, something to eat while I work, or cleaning up after," Brogan said. "I'm a master shoemaker, and I'm far too busy making shoes for half the court to do such things for myself."

Alba huddled behind a crossbeam, to make sure Moimir didn't see her from the loft. It also hid her heated cheeks, at the thought of what she and Brogan had almost done. Bedding him was one thing, but like most men of her class, he wanted a wife who would cook and clean for him.

Perhaps if her father had not had such high hopes for her, none of this would have happened. When her mother died, he'd hired a woman to cook and clean for them, and as Alba had grown, so had her interest in his work. So he'd allowed her to paint and work leather, and when her attempts to cook had turned into burned messes, she'd been allowed to stay out of the kitchen and stick with what she was good at.

Her father had wanted her to marry one of his customers, some highborn man who kept servants and had no need of a wife who could cook. Or who knew a trade, and ran a business of her own. So the shop had gone to her brothers, with his command for them to take care of her, until she married and moved on to better things.

If only her father had known they would disregard his command, or that no highborn man or merchant had ever expressed their desire to marry her, much less made an offer.

It was a good thing the guards had

interrupted when they did. Or she might have taken Brogan to bed…nay, put on the clothes he'd given her, then taken them off and taken him to bed, for without the curse broken, she'd make a poor bedfellow to a grown man. If he didn't break her in two… Oh, her cheeks burned even hotter at that thought.

She glanced at the pallet where she slept, now the subject of the guard's scrutiny.

"Does anyone else live here with you?" Moimir called down.

Brogan barely hesitated. "No, no one."

His lie shouldn't have hurt, but it did. It was a good hurt, though, reminding her that she truly was no one to him, as she should be.

"Then whose bed is this?" Moimir lifted the coverlet on her bed, and Alba's heart sank. She should never have allowed Brogan to bring such a thing up to the loft for her. It wasn't as though she slept much, anyway…

"That's for…my apprentice. Being so busy and all, I thought it was high time I took on an apprentice. Only the boy I'd expected fell ill. So, until he recovers or I choose someone else, it's just me." The brightness in Brogan's tone sounded so false, Alba was certain the guards would hear it and arrest him.

Yet they did not. Instead, they finished their search and departed, wishing Brogan a good night.

He waved them off, then shut the door and sank onto a bench, his head in his hands. After a long moment, he said, "Alba?"

She longed to answer, but pressed her lips firmly together. Their kiss had been a mistake. A delicious mistake, one to dream about in all the cold nights ahead, but still a mistake. One she would not repeat, or aggravate further by showing any more affection to Brogan.

"Alba, I'm sorry," he said softly.

Sorry. Yes. So was she. But for kissing him in the first place, or refusing to do it again…she could not say.

Forty-Eight

All too soon, Dalia stood on Brogan's doorstep, ready to put her plan into action.

Alba had already done her part, feeding her brothers the bait about the valuable wagon they might rob, and now it only remained to see if they were desperate enough to take it.

Dalia did not seem worried, sweeping into the shop as though she were queen of all the world. Well, she was a witch, and a close friend of the Queen, for she was the Princess's godmother. Dalia's eyes lit up as her gaze landed on the boots in Alba's hands. "Ah, they look magnificent," she said. "All they need is a little magic to make them perfect."

Alba drew back. She had had enough of magic to last her a lifetime.

The witch was so focused on her spell she did not notice Alba's reaction, or perhaps she did not care. The witch bit down on her lip so hard, blood welled up, but the witch paid that no heed, either. She waved her hands over the boots, repeating the gesture several times until she was satisfied. Then she gave a little nod, and said, "There. That should do it. Though I should try them out first…"

Alba swallowed. She'd spoken little in the days after her kiss with Brogan, and her voice felt gritty from disuse. "Yes, please try them on. See that they fit. If they do, you may take them with you tonight." And your shadow will never darken this door again, Alba thought but did not say.

Today, it seemed the witch could not read minds, or she was simply too busy to do so. She took off her worn boots, and slid her stockinged feet into the new pair. Then the witch stood, tapped her foot three times on the flagstone, and vanished.

Alba gasped. Brogan swore.

"Oh, I'm getting too old for that," the witch said, sounding like she was in the cellar below them. The creak of footsteps on the stairs confirmed it. "And the toes on these pinch something awful. Is there anything you can do about that?"

"I could rub them with oil, which would soften the leather somewhat," Alba said.

The witch took off her new boots and dumped them on the table before Alba. "Yes. Please do that. I will leave these with you, and wear my own, more comfortable boots for this little adventure."

"Do your other boots make you invisible, too?" Brogan asked eagerly.

Dalia snorted. "Of course they don't. Neither did the new ones. What I cast is an escape spell. You see, when I am wearing the boots, all I need to do is tap my toes three times, and a hole appears, big enough for me to slip through. It works on walls as well as floors, opening doors where there are none. Wearing these boots, you could never truly be a prisoner, for no prison cell would hold you." Her eyes met Alba's as she said this, as though her words were not meant for Brogan at all.

Perhaps the witch could read her thoughts after all. "Would such a spell allow me to leave the house, while still under your curse?" Alba asked.

The witch blinked. "No," she admitted. "The curse must be broken first but after that… Why, you could walk through the walls of the strongest castle keep as though there were no walls at all."

"Best keep those boots safe, then, Alba," Brogan said briskly. "We wouldn't want those to fall into the wrong hands before Mistress Dalia comes back to collect them."

Like her brothers' hands. Alba shivered at the thought.

But if all went according to plan, by the morrow, her brothers would be safely in a prison somewhere, unable to harm her or Brogan ever again. Their days of robbing carriages would be over.

If Dalia's plan worked.

Alba prayed it would.

Forty-Nine

When Dalia and Brogan had gone, Alba found a flask of oil and a soft cloth with which to work on Dalia's boots.

She worked the oil into the leather, wishing she knew more of the details of the witch's plan, but now it was too late to ask.

All she knew was that Dalia, Brogan and presumably a squad of guards would surprise her brothers when they tried to rob the coach. How, where, when...she did not know any of these things, for she had not asked.

When Dalia and Brogan had been making

their plans, they deliberately left her out, because Alba could not leave the house, and the less she knew, the less she could tell her brothers, if they came for her.

Alba had bridled at the distrust in the witch's tone when she said that, and resolved to ask Brogan about it later, but then they'd kissed, and she hadn't been able to work up the courage to ask about the plan. Brogan at least knew she would never help her brothers, not willingly, anyway. But the witch…

Alba slammed the witch's boot against the table, rubbing as hard as she dared at the leather. If only she could wipe the witch's suspicion off her face as easily, she fumed. After everything her brothers had put her through, why would she help them? No one wanted them brought to justice more than Alba herself.

Which was why she wished she'd swallowed her pride and asked one of them about the plan. Instead of just sitting here waiting, not knowing, worrying, wishing…

"Open this door in the name of the King!"

The guards had returned. Alba frowned. Yet

today, she'd scarcely made a sound. Certainly no screaming. Then why…

The door flew open, and two guards crowded inside.

Alba's heart sank. With all her worrying, she'd forgotten the simplest of things – she'd forgotten to bar the door.

Before the guards could stop her, she slid under the table, praying that she could hide.

A hand seized the back of her tunic, dragging her out from under the table. Something cold and sharp touched her throat.

"You're going to help us, sister, or I'll slit your throat," Onni's voice growled. "And when your shoemaker comes home, we'll kill him, too."

Alba's heart jumped into her throat, choking her. "I can't… The curse…" she began.

Onni shook her, and the blade at her throat broke the skin, stinging like he'd rubbed salt on the blade. She wouldn't put it past him.

A familiar bundle of rags lay on the table before her. "Put these on. Hurry, for we have a carriage to catch." Gad grinned.

Onni threw her on the ground, and the

bundle of rags landed beside her. "Get dressed! Now!"

Alba hurried to obey. There were more holes than cloth, and they smelled like someone had used them to clean a chamber pot. Yet one glance at Onni and his knife made her put the horrid garments on anyway.

"The shoes! Don't forget shoes!"

Alba would not call the things shoes. Someone had coarsely tacked pieces of oily cloth to two pieces of wood, presumably lashing them around their ankles and calves so the things stayed on. When they'd first been put together, these shoes – and she used the word loosely – might have lasted a week. That week was likely many years in the past, for the wood had worn so thin in places it might pass for parchment. Her feet would freeze before she crossed the street.

But if she had to choose between frozen feet or death, and worse, Brogan's death, then she would wear this travesty pretending to be a pair of shoes.

She peeled two strips off the hem of her…well, she supposed it was a skirt…and used those to bind the boots about her ankles.

The moment she finished tying the second binding, the strangest feeling came over her. Fire flooded her very bones, and she needed to stretch, or her whole body would come apart at the seams. So she did, stretching until she thought her joints would pop, and yet she did not stop. An eternity or a moment passed, she could not be sure, but finally the feeling faded.

"See? I told you!" Onni crowed. "The whorehouse will take her now!"

Whorehouse? No.

"No, I told you we need her for the job," Gad growled.

While her brothers argued, Alba peeled off the cloth shoes and reach for the witch's magical boots. They fit her perfectly, the smooth leather caressing her feet as though they'd been made for her, not the witch.

Gad thrust a threadbare cloak at her. "Here, put this on."

She barely had time to fling it about her shoulders before her brothers grabbed her arms and dragged her out into the street.

To the curious crowd outside, Onni said

that she was a dangerous thief, caught robbing the master shoemaker. They were taking her to the dungeons. The crowd parted to let them through, courtesy of the guard uniforms her brothers wore. She didn't even want to think where they'd stolen them from.

Or what fate awaited her.

At least, if she did not like it, she could use the witch's borrowed boots to escape.

Though to where, she was not sure.

Fifty

Just when Brogan thought Dalia's carriage had been bumping and rattling for an eternity, it slowed to a stop. He looked askance at Dalia.

The witch shrugged. She did not seem perturbed, so Brogan did his best to keep calm, too.

It wasn't long before the driver opened the carriage door and bowed deeply. "Mistress, we have arrived at the inn," he said.

"Ah, good," she said, allowing the driver to help her out of the carriage and down to the ground.

Brogan emerged without assistance, staring around at the near empty inn yard. No one in Kasmirus had a yard this big – therefore they were definitely outside the city, further than he had ever travelled before in his life. Brogan swallowed. He was doing this for Alba, he reminded himself. If he was too cowardly to brave the safe confines of a country inn, where would he find the courage to face down both her brothers and see them brought to justice? Alba deserved a brave man, not a coward.

The witch led the way inside, and Brogan lifted his chin as proudly as he dared, determined to follow her.

She swept through the inn's taproom, making no move to sit at any of the tables, before her progress was blocked by a woman with a curtsy so deep you would think that the witch was royalty.

She was the Princess's godmother, Brogan reflected. Perhaps the witch did have royal blood. Her clothes were not that of a courtier, but for all their plainness, they were well made. Much like the boots Alba had crafted for her, made from materials both fine and practical, yet unadorned.

He had to hurry to catch up to Dalia and the woman he suspected was the innkeeper's wife, who were already halfway up the stairs to the next level. The woman led them to a small chamber with its own fire and a table and chairs, of finer craftsmanship than those in the taproom below.

"Please, make yourself comfortable, mistress," the innkeeper's wife said. "I shall have hot cider and hunter's stew brought up. Should you have need of anything else, merely ask the maid and it shall be brought to you." Another deep curtsy, and the woman was gone.

"We're stopping for a midday meal?" Brogan asked. "What happens if our quarry overtakes us while we are wasting time here?"

The witch laughed. "Be easy, Master Shoemaker. Jarek, the driver of the salt wagon, is a man of fixed habits. Every trip, he breaks his journey at this very inn. His horses are fed and watered, and he himself partakes in a full bowl of their famous hunter's stew. Most travellers along this road do the same. If our bandits have even a lick of sense between them, having researched their target properly, they will know this is the best place at which to steal the wagon. For while Jarek is at dinner, they can hitch up the horses, and ride away. There is a crossroads a few hundred yards distant, where one road leads to the mine, and another heads south for the mountains. The moment Jarek arrives, the maid will come to tell us, we shall go keep watch by the wagon, and when the men come to steal it, we shall catch them in the act."

It sounded so simple, and Brogan wished with all his being that the witch was right. "Shouldn't we be keeping watch? What if the maids are busy, and by the time we receive word that the wagon is here, the bandits have been and gone, taking the wagon with them?"

Dalia shook her head. "This place is almost empty, with more maids than customers. At Midsummer, when the road is packed with travellers, perhaps such a thing could happen. But today? Nay, I will wager you as much gold as you make in a year that we will receive word of the wagon before the horses are even unhitched."

"You already owe me that much for those boots, for such fine leather does not come cheap," Brogan said. "But if your plan goes as smoothly as you say, then my peace of mind and Alba's safety are worth more to me than a year's pay. If you are right, then you may consider the boots a gift."

The witch nodded approvingly. "You risk much for a girl you barely know. Are you sure she is worthy of your trust?"

"Alba is nothing like her brothers. She is kind and hard-working, with not a speck of malice in her heart. Where her brothers would have burned my house down around my ears, she helped to build my business to higher heights than I could have ever dreamed possible. I owe her everything, and if it takes my whole life to repay her, then I shall make it my life's work."

The witch opened her mouth to respond, but she was interrupted by the entrance of a maid. Soon, two huge bowls of aromatic stew steamed before them, with a sizeable jug of cider and loaf of bread so large it would feed a family in addition to the two of them.

The witch breathed deeply. "This is the best hunter's stew you have ever eaten," she said with a smile. "I will not place a wager on that, for I know it is true. It is said the first time they made it was when a king slept under the roof, giving rise to the name on the sign outside – the King's Bowl. Which king, or how long ago, I do not know, but no man who can afford a bowl of hunter's stew, be he king or commoner, would pass this place by. Least of all Jarek, the driver we are waiting for." She picked up her spoon. "So savour your stew, Master Shoemaker, and perhaps if you are lucky, once we have caught our quarry, there may yet be some left in the pot for you to carry home to the girl you hold in such high esteem."

Brogan took a taste, and decided to take the witch's advice. Catching criminals was so far beyond his experience that he must bow to hers. So instead, he let himself focus on the blending of flavours and the abundance of meat in his bowl, and anticipation at Alba's joy when he brought her both good news and a good meal.

"This is perfect," Onni declared.

Huddled behind him on the undoubtedly stolen horse, Alba lifted her head to see what could possibly be perfect. All she saw was an icy road that stretched as far forward as it did back. The only difference between this spot and any other they'd stopped at was that it was on a slight rise, giving more of a view than usual.

"Get down," Onni ordered.

Alba looked about her, but there was nowhere to climb down from the horse without falling onto hard ice. "How?" she asked icily.

A fist came out of nowhere, colliding with her jaw so hard she slipped sideways, and then there was no stopping her fall. The impact knocked the breath out of her, so that all she could do was stare up at her laughing brothers. If Father could only see them now…

Onni kicked his horse, and rode out of sight, but Gad stayed, fumbling for something under his cloak. A cloak warmer than the one they'd given her, Alba fumed. What she'd give to be back in Brogan's house, sitting at the table before the fire.

After a moment, Gad produced a crossbow. A loaded crossbow, which he pointed at her. "Stay there. Don't get up, or I'll shoot you. You don't have to be alive to be bait."

Bait? So her brothers were going after the salt mine wagon. Having taken her bait…they intended her to be theirs. Oh, the irony of it. All she had to do was wait for the wagon to appear, and Brogan and Dalia would turn the tables on her brothers. She just had to survive until then.

<h1 style="text-align:center">Fifty-Two</h1>

The sound of approaching hoof beats, felt even through the ice, lifted Alba's spirits slightly before Gad's voice sank them again.

"And?" he asked.

"It's no good," Onni panted. He sucked in a breath, then continued, "Between her pale skin and the colour of her clothes, she blends right in with the road. You can't see her until you're nearly on top of her, and that's no good. If he doesn't see her, he won't stop. She needs to wear something more colourful."

Gad glared. "Well it's a bit late for that now,

isn't it? No tailors or weavers here!"

Gad reached for his water skin and drank deeply. Onni's eyes lit up.

"Here, give me that," Onni said, stretching out his hand.

Gad hesitated for only a moment, before he handed it over. "What's wrong with yours?"

Onni upended the water skin, squirting the contents all over Alba.

She let out a yelp of protest as the cold liquid drenched her already ruined clothes. The strong smell of wine made her dizzy, but she waited until she was certain the skin was empty before daring to open her eyes. Her grey rags were now stained dark red, sticky and cold against her skin. If she made it out of this alive, she was going to drag the old dye bath up from the cellar, and heat enough water to have a proper bath.

Gad has that crossbow in his hands again, aiming it unsteadily at her. "You stay there," he commanded. He pointed a thick finger at his brother. "You go see if she is visible from the road now."

Onni grumbled, but his horse's hoof beats

said he'd obeyed anyway.

It seemed a much shorter time until he returned.

"Hide! Hide! It's coming!" Onni hissed. Then there came the sound of snapping branches as he and his horse headed into the woods by the side of the road.

Gad hung back. "Don't you move," he said. "I'll be watching you, and if you so much as twitch wrong… I'll put a bolt in you. Don't you think I won't." Then he and his horse were gone, too.

Before the curse, Alba might have talked herself into believing that her brothers did not mean to shoot her. Now? Now she knew they were deadly serious.

Well, she could make vows, too. Onni and Gad were her brothers no longer. They might have been family once, but they were nothing to her now.

The rumble of more traffic along the road had her holding her breath, praying that her ordeal was finally at an end.

Now she could discern hoof beats from more than one horse, along with the dull vibration of the wagon behind.

An unfamiliar voice called to the horses to halt. Obediently, they did.

The thump of heavy boots landing on the ice was close enough for her to feel it in her very bones. A big man, well fed and wearing good boots.

Much like the silk clad beast who'd pinned her beneath his monstrous bulk as he battered his way through her maidenhead, splattering blood on the road. Like a newly forged sword thrust deep in her insides, she'd screamed at the pain until…

"By all that's holy, what are you doing here?" The man wore so much fur that, at first glance, Alba thought he was part bear.

"Help," she said, her voice weak. She cleared her throat and tried again. "Please help me."

"Of course," he said. Off came the thickly furred cloak, before he helped her to her feet. He wrapped the heavy garment around her twice before lifting her up to the seat at the front of the wagon. "You look just like my daughter Maria," he said. "What's your name, girl?"

"Alba," she said, having no need to lie.

"I'm Jarek," he said. "I have a skin of strong wine that I'd planned on bringing home, but I think you might need some to warm you up." His eyes held nothing but sympathy as he took her in. "I'll go get it, and then we'll be underway again."

He disappeared around the side of the wagon, and Alba allowed herself a moment to relax. He'd open the wagon, the witch would hop out, and her brothers wouldn't be able to hurt anyone ever again.

Thunk.

"Aw, you didn't need to kill him!" Onni complained.

No, not Brogan!

Alba twisted around in her seat, in time to see Jarek crumple to the ground, a crossbow bolt sticking out of his throat. He gurgled as blood bubbled from the wound, before an ominous silence fell.

Behind him, the wagon door was still barred.

"We better get out of here quick, before

anyone knows we did this," Gad said.

Onni nodded slowly. "Get up on the wagon. It'll be faster."

Alba found herself squeezed between her two brothers barely a moment before Onni snapped the whip over the horses to make them move again.

"Aren't you going to check what's inside the wagon?" she asked.

"Not until we're far away from that," Onni replied, plying the whip again.

They crested the hill and a gust of wintry wind caught them. With only her face exposed, Alba was glad of the fur cloak, though she wished its owner sat beside her instead of her brothers.

"Hey, that's much too big for you. Give it to me!" Onni tugged at her cloak, nearly throwing her off the wagon in his haste to claim her gift for himself. Never mind that he had his own cloak, while hers had been left behind on the road when she'd fallen from his horse.

All too soon, she had nothing but sodden rags to protect her from the freezing wind.

"Stop squirming!" Gad ordered.

"I'm not squirming, I'm shivering, and I can't stop. I'm too cold!" Alba said. "Onni took my cloak."

"My cloak now," the bastard gloated.

"Let me ride inside, out of the wind," she said. "Then I won't…bother you." Or freeze to death, not that they cared about that. Her only hope was to get the door open and release the only people who would help her.

Onni yanked on the reins, dragging the horses to a stop. "Fine. But if you're thinking of stealing anything…"

Alba held up her hands. They had begun to turn blue. "I'm not, I swear."

"Put her inside, and lock the door so she can't escape," Onni ordered.

Now it was Gad's turn to grumble as he dragged her down from the seat to the side of the wagon. He unbarred the door, opening it just wide enough to shove her inside, before slamming it shut again. The bar clunked down a moment later, trapping her in the darkness.

"Hello? Brogan, Dalia?" she whispered, exploring the darkness with her hands in the hope of touching something that wasn't made of wood.

But there was no answer, and the wagon began moving again, throwing her against a wall of what felt like casks. Something round and wooden, anyway.

"Brogan? Dalia? Anybody?"

But there was no answer.

Fifty-Three

Alba explored the cramped space as best she could in the dark. Most of the space was taken up by casks on one side and wooden boxes on the other, stacked from floor to ceiling. If there had been three people in there, it would have been a tight squeeze.

As it was, with just her there, she found what felt like an almost empty sack and sat on it to cushion her against the rough ride. If her brothers didn't manage to shake the wagon to pieces before they reached their destination, she'd be surprised. Surely they'd break a wheel or an axle or some such thing. Though whether the boxes or the barrels would crush her first seemed her more pressing problem.

So much for Dalia's help. She knew she shouldn't have trusted the witch. Brogan would have helped her if he could, but if the witch misled him, he could be miles away, and no use to her.

Well, the witch wouldn't be getting her boots, then, Alba mused. And if the witch wanted to hunt her down for stealing them, then she was welcome to try. For when she saw the witch next, Alba would not be holding her tongue. Nor returning the boots. They were her work, some of her best, and she'd brought in enough money for Brogan not to begrudge her the leather for them.

And the boots had broken the curse, despite Dalia's words to the contrary. Even witches were wrong sometimes.

Of course, it had to be the one time Alba didn't want her to be wrong…

Laughter bubbled up so hard she could no longer contain it. What with the rattling, rumbling wagon, her brothers wouldn't hear it, anyway. She laughed so hard, drumming her feet on the floor until her feet felt numb. Or like there was no floor beneath them…

Alba remembered too late about the bespelled boots. She dropped through the hole in the floor, narrowly missing the rear wheels as she tumbled to the road, rolling across the rutted ice until she came to a stop in a ditch beside the road.

Something heavy sat on her chest, making it hard to breathe even if she hadn't felt black and blue and bruised all over. She lifted her head to look, and found the sack she'd been sitting on had turned the tables. It wasn't empty, either – inside was a squashed loaf of bread and a water skin.

Her mouth tasted of blood from where she'd undoubtedly bitten her tongue in her fall from the wagon. Alba uncorked the skin and drank deeply.

Fire burned down her throat, setting her insides ablaze. Jarek's strong wine, not water at all. She silently thanked the man for his kindness and foresight – she did indeed need this. But perhaps she could still thank him – if he lived, she could help him, and if he didn't, perhaps she could at least see he had a decent burial. And that the city guards knew who slew him.

She ripped a hole in the sack, wide enough to poke her head through, then one more so that one of her arms was free. She took another gulp of warmth from her wineskin to fortify her, and set off back the way she'd come.

Oblivious to her escape, the wagon driven by her brothers bounced away behind her.

Fifty-Four

A maid burst into the room, panting like she'd raced up the stairs. "Mistress Dalia, it's Jarek and the salt wagon," she said. "Only he's got someone with him. Hard to tell who, they're going so fast. And they don't look like they're slowing down."

Dalia rose. "Have my carriage made ready immediately. Brogan, it's time."

Finally. Brogan followed the maid down the steps, running out into the yard. Only then did he realise Dalia wasn't behind him.

He debated whether to go back inside for

her, but decided to stay with her carriage instead. The horses still had to be harnessed up to it, and her coachman would hardly leave without her.

By the time the witch did appear, everything was ready and waiting, and all she had to do was step into the carriage before they set out.

"Do you want me to catch them, mistress?" the coachman asked eagerly.

"No, I want a smooth ride, please, Konstanty. A steady pace, but not too fast," she responded.

"But they'll get away!" Brogan protested.

The look Dalia turned toward him would have frightened a much braver man. But all Brogan's fear was fixed on what her brothers might do to Alba if he let them go free. He had nothing left to make him quail before the witch.

"They will not. The fools are whipping their horses into a frenzy to go so fast. I saw the wagon – it's a miracle it hasn't shaken itself to pieces already. Though perhaps one of those poor horses might die first. Either way, they will be waiting for us on the road when we arrive. If they're fool enough, they may try to take this carriage, too." She sniffed. "Hanging is too good for them."

Brogan would be happy to see them hang, if only to make sure Alba never suffered at their hands again.

They did not need to go far. They found one horse dead just past the crossroads, and the wagon with the second dead horse only a mile further along.

"Stay inside the carriage unless I call for you," the witch ordered.

Brogan opened his mouth to protest. Witch she might be, but he'd never heard of a woman besting two men in a fight. Alba's brothers were brigands, and surely knew how to fight better than she.

"Be quiet, or I will send you to sleep on the floor of the carriage until this is over," Dalia said. "Don't underestimate an enchantress. Especially not one with the sight. You will do as I say if you want to go home with that girl of yours, and make babies with her."

Brogan's cheeks burned. He hadn't been thinking of such things, but when she spoke of them, the most distracting pictures popped into his head.

"Konstanty, you're to stop well away from them. Climb down and approach the downed wagon, to see if anyone needs help. When you are far enough away, then they'll spring their ambush. I will be ready," Dalia said.

"As you wish, mistress." The burly coachman didn't seem the slightest bit worried about his mistress. Perhaps she was as powerful as she said. Konstanty hailed the downed wagon, his voice growing fainter as he got further away.

Without warning, Dalia jumped to her feet, shouldered open the door and jumped out of her carriage. "No you don't!" she shouted. Something thumped to the ground outside the carriage, followed by a second thump, heavier than the first. After a long pause, she said, "Master Shoemaker, you may come out now."

Trying not to look like he'd been cowering in the carriage during combat, or whatever had occurred outside while he'd been sitting there, waiting for her summons, Brogan stuck his head through the door. What he saw was enough to reassure him into stepping out onto the road.

Two men lay facedown on the ice, though the one under the bearskin cloak was only identifiable as a person by the shoe peeking out from under the voluminous folds. Dalia stood over them with a look of disgust on her face.

"Take the fur cloak and the crossbow. These two won't be riding inside with us. Konstanty, help me tie them to the roof."

Obediently, Brogan bundled the massive cloak up in his arms, taking it to the carriage, before returning for the crossbow. Dalia stretched her hands out, palms up, before her, and the two men began to float from the road to the roof.

Brogan stopped, fascinated. He'd never seen magic performed like this before, and it was wondrous to behold.

"Use plenty of rope," Dalia advised her coachman, who now stood on the driver's seat, his hands resting on the roof, ready to receive his charges. "I don't think they'll break this spell so easily without their sister to help them, but there's no trusting tricksters like these. Make sure you tie them tightly."

The coachman made quick work of his task, and they were soon underway again, this time toward the salt mine.

Dalia stroked the cloak with sadness in her eyes. "Jarek did not deserve this fate. I had thought to deliver justice but now...I'm not sure they have enough years left to live for justice to truly make up for what they have done today."

She said little more until they arrived at the salt mine, a place that looked more like a village than a mine.

When a man approached to ask their business, Dalia asked to speak to the head overseer, or whoever was in charge. Things moved swiftly, then – the two men were dragged down from the roof and marched into a low building with barred windows, while he and Dalia followed a well-armed guard into the Great House.

"Lord Salinas, this is Mistress Dalia the Enchantress, and Master Shoemaker Brogan of Kasmirus." The guard bowed, gesturing for them to enter the chamber beyond.

Brogan walked into a low room not unlike the taproom in the King's Bowl, though it lacked a bar and the crowd of patrons he would expect in an inn.

The lone man inside didn't look like a lord — at least, not like the courtiers she'd seen in his shop. He was dressed like a man who worked for a living, but in a trade that paid well. Presumably, salt mining did.

"Mistress Dalia, Master Brogan. Please, sit. Have some wine." Lord Salinas gestured to the bench opposite him, as a servant rushed forward to set out cups and a fresh jug of wine. "We get few visitors here, particularly in the winter months. If you have come from Kasmirus, do you bring urgent word from the King?" He drank from his own cup. "My own man, Jarek, was supposed to leave Kasmirus today. He could have carried your message and saved you the trouble."

"I regret being the bearer of bad tidings, but Jarek met with ill fortune on the road from Kasmirus. The two men who visited it upon him are now locked in your cells. Because of this and…other crimes they have committed, I wish to question them, and ask your help in ensuring that they meet with suitable justice."

Lord Salinas spread out his hands. "How can I be of service?"

Fifty-Five

Even when Alba's brothers were manacled hand and foot, still Brogan didn't trust them not to try to escape. So while the witch questioned them, he stood by, with Lord Salinas standing in silent judgement beside him.

"You've got the wrong men, mistress," Onni said, his voice high and righteous. "This is all our sister's fault, as wicked a woman as you would find anywhere. As if Eve and Jezebel were born again within a single woman's body, armed with the devil's own seductive tongue."

Alba? Brogan snorted softly. They could not be speaking of the same girl.

"Tell me about your sister," Dalia instructed.

"Well, it was all fine when Father was alive. We all worked hard in his shoemaking business, the place now owned by Brogan over there." Onni pointed.

Brogan shrank against the wall. He wanted no part in this story.

"He was the Royal Shoemaker, a master at his trade, and we were well off, but it was not enough for Alba. She fancied herself as good as any of the ladies who came into the shop, putting on airs and wanting to wear silk everyday like she was in court. She planned to seduce some lord into falling in love with her, so that she might live in a castle like a queen." Onni took a deep breath. "Oh, she was beautiful on the outside, but she had a wicked, wicked heart. Every coin we worked so hard to earn, she spent on silks and furs. Our father loved her so much, he worked himself to death to give the girl what she wanted. His dying wish was for Gad and me to provide for her, just as he had. Of course, being dutiful sons, we could not deny him, and promised to take care of her.

"We worked and worked, but two of us could not earn enough at shoemaking to satisfy her appetite for finery, and she demanded more. When courtiers came past, she would point at the carriages and clothes, and insist upon having whatever it was that the noblewomen had.

"At last, unable to bear her nagging, at her command, we took a chest of clothes and jewels from a carriage that she swore was hers, but had been stolen from her tailor. But even that was not enough for her voracious appetite.

"Despite working all day and night, we could no longer afford food or rent, and our landlord evicted us. Forced to leave the city, we found shelter at a cottage in the woods beside the road. Day after day, Alba would watch the carriages go past, raging at all the finery we had been forced to leave behind that she could see noblewomen wearing. She insisted we must stop the carriages, and demand they return her things."

Onni buried his face in his hands and gave a great sob. "To my great sorrow, we did."

"We soon began to suspect that her tongue was forked, that she lied about owning so many things, for the nobles in their carriages claimed they were being robbed, calling us bandits and other such things. But when we suggested this to her, she flew into a rage, screaming that we had promised Father to take care of her, and if we were to break an oath made to a man on his deathbed, then we would surely go to hell."

Onni sniffed. "I feared for her soul, but I feared for my own more, so I did as she bade me. Gad was quicker to see the truth of it than me. One morning, when she raged at a new carriage that had appeared on the road, he set upon her with a rod, determined to beat the evil out of her. He beat her until her fine clothes shredded, but still the devil would not leave her. Finally, his arms grew too tired to lift, and she screamed that she would claim her property herself if we were not man enough to do it.

"You probably remember that day, mistress.

She ran up to your carriage, her clothes hanging in ribbons, but she had no care for her modesty like a normal woman might. Instead, she begged for your help. Help she did not deserve, as you saw so clearly, when you cursed her."

Brogan found himself shaking his head at such vicious lies. This was nothing like the Alba he knew, or the history she'd told him. It couldn't be true. Couldn't be.

"What about today? How came you to be on the salt wagon today?" Dalia asked, her voice flat and calm as though she heard tales like this every day. Surely she couldn't believe them.

"After the curse, all that we owned – all her finery – disappeared. She found a way to break the curse, with the help of a simple-minded shoemaker, but she refused to leave him until she'd managed to seduce the location of her missing things from him. When faced with such a beautiful woman…he was no match for her womanly wiles, and he told her everything. Then she told us it would be in a wagon travelling along the road to the mountains today. All we had to do was wait for it to come past and take it back for her.

"But when she saw the wagon, she went mad. She screamed that the man driving it had stolen her fur cloak, and she produced a crossbow, which she must have concealed about her person somehow, and shot him dead. Then she proceeded to take the cloak off his corpse. Of course, it was too big for her to carry, so Gad, quick thinking man that he is, overpowered her while she was distracted, and commanded me to open the wagon so we might lock her inside. She screamed curses at us through the door, beating her fists and likely her feet against it, too, but she could not escape."

He drew in a great, jagged breath. "And so, we took responsibility for the murdered man's coach, seeing as his murderer was safely locked inside, and drove it to the nearest town, where we hoped someone would be willing to mete out justice for the murderess we have the misfortune to call our sister."

"Where is she now?" Dalia asked.

"Still locked in the wagon, I'd wager," Gad

said sourly. "We were only bringing her to justice, doing the right thing, when you took us prisoner without letting us utter a word in our defence. She's the real villain here. You should have taken her!"

Brogan's breath caught in his throat as the man's words sank in. Somehow, they'd managed to kidnap Alba and lock her away, and he'd left her there on the road. She had to be terrified.

"I'll go get her," he heard himself say.

"Take my carriage. Konstanty will drive you. I must finish questioning these two, and break the news to Jarek's daughter." Dalia looked grim.

Lord Salinas piped up, "I can send a squad of my guards with you. If this woman is as dangerous as they say, you may have need of them."

For one heartsick moment, Brogan wondered if there was any truth in Alba's brothers' words. If she were truly the devil incarnate as they said…

"My coachman is more than capable of subduing an unarmed girl half his size. Sending two men is more than enough," Dalia said drily. "Why, the Master Shoemaker alone is capable of seeing to the girl. Is that not so, Master Brogan?"

"Yes, of course," he replied, his thoughts whirling. If she was innocent, he would not let anyone else near her. He would protect her with his life, as he'd promised. If she was guilty...why, he would be honour-bound to bring her to justice, as well as shamed for having let her fool him, too.

He needed to speak to her, to hear the truth from her own lips. Every word she'd told him rang true, while her brothers' falsehoods left a sour taste in his mouth.

Fifty-Six

Darkness had fallen by the time they reached the wagon. The dead horse was still harnessed to it, and Brogan blessed the frigid air for freezing the animal before it had started to smell. The wagon had canted over toward the corpse, so it took the efforts of the two of them to heft open the door.

Inside lay a jumble of casks and crates. Brogan held his torch high, looking for some sign of Alba, but the wagon's cargo had evidently buried her from sight.

"Help me shift these. She must be

underneath, somewhere. If they haven't crushed her..." Brogan worked feverishly to lift things out of the wagon, which Konstanty set on the road.

He lifted until his arms ached, and then he lifted some more, because if Alba was alive under there, he had to save her. Finally, he had to admit the truth: she was not in the wagon at all.

His heart swelled with joy. Her brothers had lied. He knew it! Alba was safely at home, and with her brothers in the mine prison, she would finally be free of them.

"This is strange," Konstanty said, holding up what looked like a bracelet. "It looks like one of the silken ribbons girls wear at court, but it's made of leather."

Brogan snatched it from him, examining the thong in the light of his torch. It had been tied around something, then finished with a bow — precisely like Alba tied off her braided hair. He rubbed the leather between his fingers — definitely good quality, well-worked with the kind of softness preferred by court ladies. He untied it, and traced the edge of the strip of leather. One side was cut straight across, but the other had a curve to it, like it was one of the scraps sitting on the table after he'd cut a shoe. Except that the curve was more precise than anything he'd ever cut. No, this had been cut by the hand of a true master of the craft. The sort he watched at work every night. He didn't want to believe it, but…

"She was here. But she must have escaped somehow…" Even as the words left his lips, Brogan didn't believe them. It had taken two men to open the wagon door – Alba could not have lifted it. Unless she'd made her escape while the wagon was moving…

Brogan wet his lips. "We should head back to the city, and search the road." The witch would have ordered her coachman to do what she wanted, but Brogan was Konstanty's equal, not his superior. And if the witch had given the man different orders, Brogan doubted Konstanty would deviate from Dalia's approved course of action.

"Mistress Dalia said you know her best, and she wants the girl found. You might want to come sit up front with me. Two pairs of eyes are better than one, when searching in the dark." Konstanty winked. "And you'll want to take one of the furs from inside the carriage, to keep you warm. Riding in the driver's seat is not like walking – the wind chills you, instead of the effort making you warm."

Gratefully, Brogan took the coachman's advice, and they set off again, peering into the dark. Brogan prayed she wanted to be found, for if she hid in the woods, with the temperature dropping rapidly…she might freeze before morning.

Fifty-Seven

Alba wasn't sure what she hated more – the endless road, the chilly winter air that bit through her thin clothes, or the sour smell of Gad's cheap wine which made her queasy.

It was the smell, she finally decided. The witch's borrowed boots were the most comfortable shoes she'd ever worn, not to mention warm, and Jarek's wine helped her with the cold. But the stench permeated everything.

A stream ran beside the road, taunting her about her wish to have a bath. The water would be icy, but her roiling stomach told her it would be worth it. She needn't immerse herself – just wash off the wine.

The sun was sinking by the time she gave in to temptation. She stripped off the wine-soaked rags and used one of the cleaner patches to scrub the stickiness from her skin. She put the boots back on, and the sack, but she left the wet rags where they lay. It wasn't like they were much protection against the cold. Instead, she took a mouthful of Jarek's wine and continued along the road.

Slowly, feeling came back into her toes, and then her fingers. She wished she could wash the wine from her hair, too, but that would have to wait until she could dry it before a fire. A comb wouldn't have gone amiss, either, for she could feel her braid unravelling. She must have lost the piece of leather she preferred to tie it with somewhere along the way – likely when Gad had thrown her into the wagon, or perhaps when she'd first landed on the road. Never mind. She could cut another one from the next pair of shoes she made.

If there was a next pair of shoes…

Of course there would be. She would keep walking until she reached Kasmirus, and the work waiting for her in Brogan's house. She'd stoke the fire, find some more suitable clothes, and return to her work until he came home.

After that…the future was uncertain, but Brogan would not begrudge her her tools, with which she still might make a living. Somewhere. If there was another shoemaker willing to take on a girl apprentice…

But she would worry about that later. Now, she forced herself to put one foot in front of the other, folding her arms across her chest to keep the warmth in from an occasional sip of strong wine, and focus on not losing her footing in the dark.

She counted her steps aloud, for there was no one to hear her.

At two thousand, full dark fell and she had to stretch her hands out before her to make sure she stayed on the road, not wandering into the forest.

At five thousand, the wineskin slipped out from where she'd tucked it under her arm, and it took her some minutes and plenty of swearing before she found it again in the dark.

At six thousand, she slipped on the ice and resolved to drink the wine more sparingly, for she could not afford to fall again. If she knocked herself unconscious, she might freeze by morning.

At nine thousand, the moon rose, lighting her way just enough for her to see that she still kept to the road.

At eleven thousand, she drained the last few drops from the wineskin. Yet still the road stretched on.

Just before she reached thirteen thousand, she thought she heard horses on the road behind her.

She almost laughed.

So many times, her brothers had forced her to seek help from random travellers on the road. Now she was free of them, the first thing she might have to do was stop a carriage and ask for help. Not knowing whether the traveller was a lust-crazed beast or a kind man, like Jarek. One thing was certain, whether she managed to get their attention or not: she would not be robbing or killing anyone tonight. No, that was her brothers' trade, not hers. Her trade was in shoes, and with her own feet as her witness, she made the best boots on this side of the mountains. Perhaps even between the mountains and the sea, for the king's kingdom stretched that far.

Now, should she try to hail the carriage, or should she hide in the woods until it had passed?

The carriage crested a rise, all lit up with lanterns like the cathedral at Christmas. All she had to do was step back off the road, among the trees, and they would never see her…

"Alba! Alba!"

No, they couldn't be calling her name. No man she knew owned a carriage. Well, the witch did, but…

"Wait, I think I see something! Slow down!"

That was Brogan's voice, she was sure of it. Or she was dreaming, her wishes fuelled by the wine and the cold. Nevertheless, Alba stood still, waiting and wishing.

If she was wrong, she could start walking again when the carriage had gone past.

"There! Stop!"

A faceless shadow climbed down from the wagon, a silhouette that spoke with Brogan's voice. "Alba? Is it really you?"

She opened her mouth, but her voice had died somewhere along the road, and she hadn't even noticed. So she nodded, hoping he could see.

He took off his cloak, and it became a swirling shadow that engulfed her in warmth. Warmth that would take life from him, even as it gave it to her.

"No, stop," she managed to say, trying to push him and the cloak away. "They'll kill you for helping me. Like they killed him…"

The cloak only tightened about her. No, arms tightened about her, lifting her up. Like a princess in some story. But she was no princess, and her story was no fairytale.

"No, Brogan, they'll kill you…they said if I didn't come with them, didn't help them, they'd lie in wait and kill you…and me, too. He had a crossbow. Gad had a crossbow. Was going to shoot me. Shot the kind bear instead…Jarek. Said he had a daughter. Only wanted to help me…"

He didn't let go. Instead, he leaned in and said, "Your brothers are both in prison cells in the salt mine. They can't hurt you any more."

"Not my brothers any more. No family of mine," she said, even as the tears spilled over. Tears she could not seem to stop.

Brogan didn't seem to mind. He carried her into the carriage, out of the wind, and the door closed behind him.

"Where to, Master Brogan?"

"Home. I'm taking her home," Brogan said.

The carriage began to move.

Fifty-Eight

Brogan almost didn't believe his eyes when he saw a ghostly figure walking beside the road. She was too tall to be Alba, he thought, before his brain caught up and he remembered that she could not have left the house without breaking the curse. She was no longer the tiny elfin waif who'd felt like a child in his arms. She was a woman grown, a woman he loved and wanted. A woman he would protect from the witch and her brothers and anyone else who tried to harm her.

He climbed down from the carriage before

it had stopped, not wanting to wait. In the lantern light, she looked like little more than a ghost, clad in a coarse sack, just like the first time he'd seen her. But this time, her head reached his shoulder, and when he wrapped his cloak around her, the curves he felt beneath the heavy wool were everything he could ever want in a woman.

She babbled nonsense about her brothers and danger, tears pouring down her cheeks. One thing was certain – she'd been through a terrible ordeal. An ordeal he'd tried to save her from, and failed. He intended to make it up to her now, though – tonight, and every day for the rest of his life.

The reassuring weight of her in his arms as he carried her to the witch's carriage made his heart sing. She was a real woman, no longer a waif, and he would save her. It wasn't too late.

They were closer to Kasmirus than the mine, so he asked Konstanty to take them home. If the witch wanted her, she could come and get her. Both of them, because Brogan wasn't leaving Alba again.

"So cold. Need to get out of…this…"

She struggled to take off the sack with her frozen fingers, and Brogan hurried to help her, grabbing a blanket to shield her modesty while she stripped off. When she was securely wrapped in the warmest fur he could find, he pulled her into his lap and draped his cloak around them both.

"You'll warm up faster this way," he said.

She nodded, squirming until she'd managed to curl up against his chest, her bottom resting perilously on his groin. If it wasn't for the thick furs between them, she'd be able to feel…

Blood rushed to his cheeks, too.

Her gaze fixed on him, reading his very soul. "I didn't think you'd come for me," she said softly. "When my brothers took me, I couldn't even leave a note to say goodbye. I'm sorry." A new tear trickled down her cheek.

Brogan wiped this one away. "No, I'm sorry I left you there without anyone to protect you. I should have stayed. The witch didn't need my help. My place was with you. I didn't realise it until today, but I truly am lost without you. I know you haven't been free of the curse for very long, and you may not have an answer for some time, but I wish to make my wishes known. I want you to be my wife, Alba. Let me protect you always, and be the family you deserve."

She lowered her eyes. "You deserve a better wife than me, Brogan. One who can cook and keep your house and…all the things a good wife should be able to do. I cannot cook, and I get so lost in my work I forget to clean or any of the other things a good wife should do. The only thing I am good at is making shoes, and my father and my brothers made it abundantly clear that it will never be enough. I'm a girl and I will never be the shoemaker he was. Never…"

Brogan couldn't help it. He chuckled. "You make shoes so beautiful, they drive the King's court crazy over them. Your father and your brothers, even me, will never equal your skill. It would be a crime, nay a tragedy, for you to do anything else. Marry me, and my shop is yours. Make as many shoes as you wish, and take me as your apprentice, so that maybe one day I'll be able to make something half as good as you. There are women enough in town willing to cook and clean for a few coins, including among our neighbours – hire whoever you please. I will give you anything you want, if only to have you as my wife."

She raised her head. "And what about love? Could you love someone like me, Brogan? A girl who cannot do women's work, whose only worth is making pretty trifles for courtiers?"

He didn't hesitate. "I do love you, Alba, and I will love you until I draw my last breath. You have given me everything – a business where I had nothing, a home where there were only ghosts, and courage to do things a lowly shoemaker should not even dream of doing. Why, for you, I was willing to fight bandits. With you at my side…I'd take on a dragon!" And probably lose, so it was a good thing dragons did not exist. "Marry me, Alba. I will love, protect and give you anything you ask for, for as long as I live."

Fifty-Nine

Three times he'd asked her to marry him, so she could not have misheard. Even after she'd confessed she could not cook, he still wanted her. She shifted in his lap, the unmistakable hardness beneath her telling her he wanted her as a woman, not just for her shoemaking skills.

She'd nearly died so many times in the last day — was lucky to be alive at all. When her father had wished she'd meet a man who wanted to marry her in his shop, he hadn't meant another shoemaker, but what her father wanted no longer mattered.

For once, someone was asking what she wanted.

She moved once more, so that she was facing Brogan, her breasts pressed against his chest through the fur. "Yes," she said. "Yes, I will marry you."

Then she took his face in her hands and kissed him, just like they had before the guards had interrupted them. There was no one to interrupt them now, though, and she was no longer the tiny, cursed elf she'd been then.

Somehow, her desires seemed to have grown along with her body, and she knew Brogan felt the same.

Why wait?

She tugged at her furs, until none remained between them, then lifted the hem of his tunic so her flesh touched his. By all that was holy, it was like being bathed in fire. She wanted him, so much.

"Are you trying to seduce me?" Brogan asked, his voice hoarse.

"I…" She felt her cheeks redden. "I'm doing a clumsy job of it, aren't I? I've never tried to seduce someone before. It's not as easy as making shoes, is it?"

"With practice, it might be. We will have all our lives together to find out."

Though his words urged caution, his body wanted her as urgently as she needed him.

"I want to feel loved. Now. I don't want to wait until the wedding. I want…you." She stared up into his desire darkened eyes. "Show me how you will love me."

"As you wish."

His hands slid slowly down her body to her hips, angling her ever so slightly toward him. An unspoken question begged her from the depths of his eyes.

"Yes," she whispered, then repeated, louder, as the hard heat of him filled her, so deep. Better than strong wine, he warmed her from within like nothing else. She didn't want anyone or anything else. Just him. The sheer joy of his touch, thrusting inside her even as it pushed her deeper into pleasure she hadn't believed possible. "Don't stop."

Sixty

Alba woke in Brogan's bed, stretching muscles that had seen more use in one night than they had in years. They'd made love twice in the carriage, and again when they reached Brogan's bed, and now she could feel him stirring beside her, the desire to do it a fourth time was all she could think about.

"Oh, Alba," he sighed with pleasure as she sank down on top of him, his body moving with hers as though they were one.

It was nearly noon by the time they climbed down from the loft. Brogan stirred the fire into life, while Alba searched through his clothes for something that might fit her. Everything else he'd bought her was now much too small. Perhaps if she bore him a daughter one day, the girl might wear those fine clothes. Alba herself would certainly never fit into them again.

She stared at the shoes she'd been making yesterday, but could not summon the will to work on them now. Instead, she set about cleaning the witch's boots, the ones she'd borrowed. They would never be new again, but she might be able to make them look nearly new. She oiled them and she rubbed them, but it was no use. She would need to make another pair for the witch.

Then Brogan brought breakfast from the bakery, and all Alba could think about was how long it had been since she'd last eaten. But it no longer mattered. She had him, and a home here, and it was almost too good to be true.

Of course it was.

The clop of a horse's hooves outside slowed, then stopped. A customer.

Alba rose from her seat and headed for the loft, to hide. Once they were married, and she had some suitable clothes, she could meet Brogan's customers, but until then…she would pretend to be a ghost again. So she crouched down in the darkness of the loft, and listened.

The door opened, then slammed shut. "I've come for my boots, and to see our business concluded. Where is she?" Dalia demanded.

"I will not tell you until you swear to me you will not take her away from here against her will."

Why would the witch do that? If her brothers were in prison, she had nothing to fear any more. If they weren't…

Alba climbed down. "Where are they?"

"I won't let you take her!" Brogan shouted. "She's innocent, I'd swear it on my life!"

"Did you ask her?" The witch's words hung in the air, heavy with suspicion and light on mercy.

Alba did not expect mercy. Last night had been more than she had any right to expect. She didn't wait for him to ask. "No, I am not innocent. If I had not agreed to go with them last night, Gad might not have brought a crossbow. Jarek might not have helped me, and he might still live. I might have been dead, with Brogan's blood on my hands, too, though I have never killed anyone, and hope never to need to. I helped my brothers distract the travellers they meant to rob, because then they wouldn't hurt anyone, and maybe they wouldn't hurt me, either. If I had not helped Brogan after my brothers burned this house, they would not have been set free, to prey on innocent people once more. I have committed no crime, but I have stood by and watched them happen, doing nothing to stop them, because if I did, I knew I would be their next victim.

"Perhaps I was innocent once, before my father died, but he left me in the care of my brothers, and in so doing, destroyed any innocence I might have known. An innocent has not seen what I have seen, has not been subject to the torment I have known, have not feared for their life at every turn. Until last night, when, for a brief moment, I felt a mite of relief when I believed justice had finally caught up with the men I once called my brothers." If they had escaped from prison, then they would come for her blood, believing she had betrayed them. If last night was her last, she would die happy. "So I ask you, witch, after all I have done, after enduring years of being confined to the same house as my tormenters by your curse, after what you claim to owe me, where are they?"

Dalia closed her eyes. She seemed to shrink, bowing her head as she bit her lip. "They will spend the rest of their lives in the salt mines."

"Until they find a way out of that, too," Alba finished for her.

"The only way out is death. A mixture of magic and more mundane methods, this time, for you are not the only one who deserves justice here. Jarek was well-liked, and the overseers would have been happy to see your brothers hang for their crimes. So, they are confined to the mines, where they must work every day of their lives, or they will not live to see the morrow. And if they try to escape…the overseers get to mete out their own justice. They will work harder than any shoemaker, and they will never see the sun again."

Slowly, Alba nodded. It was a fitting punishment, she supposed. The King's laws rewarded brigandry with death, but Dalia's form of justice seemed fairer, somehow. After everything they had done…a lifetime of labour suited them.

"Then I have a gift for you," Alba said. She took the boots from the table and held them out. "I borrowed them when my brothers took me from here, and walked many miles in them. They are no longer new, but they are still your boots. Without the spell upon them, I might have been caught with my brothers, and punished for their crimes yet again."

Dalia took the boots. "Thank you. I foresee I will have a good use for them in the future, but that is another's tale. Curses and water wheels, and spinning straw into gold. Perhaps they may even save another mother and her babe from harm. I have a gift for you, too. A name, for the child you carry, though you did not know it yet. You must call the boy George, for dragonslaying is in his blood."

This drew a surprised reaction from Brogan,

but he waved for the witch to continue.

"George, or, as they say it in the common tongue here, Jarek."

Fitting indeed. "Thank you. If we have a baby boy, that's what we'll call him."

Dalia produced a small sack that clinked, then tossed it onto the table. "I lost a wager to Master Brogan, and those are his winnings."

Neither Alba nor Brogan touched the bag of coins.

"Now there is the matter of the debt I owe you, Mistress Alba. Three, by your count. What would you ask of me?"

It was on the tip of Alba's tongue to say she needed nothing from the witch, but even as she opened her mouth, she knew it would not be true.

Alba took a deep breath. "I would ask you…should anything happen to me, or to Brogan, or if he is far from home and we cannot…please, watch over our children, so that no son or daughter of mine shares my fate."

Dalia considered for a moment. "You ask me to be godmother to your child? The one thing you ask, and I cannot grant it. Because I will only grow older, and if I have made mistakes before, who knows when I shall make more? I am not a good choice for godmother. Even the Crown Princess…but I cannot speak of that yet, for what is to come may change, though much rides on her future. A future that is entwined with that of your son, too. I will offer you something better. Name my own daughter, Zoraida, as your child's godmother. She is young and strong, and may be more use if your son should encounter any dragons."

"Our son will be a shoemaker. If he is lucky, he will be as good as his mother," Brogan said. "He'll be sensible enough to leave slaying of dragons and other such monsters to knights and those who have the training for it."

Dalia covered her mouth with her hand, but Alba saw the smile she hid from Brogan. Alba wondered what the witch knew that they did not. It mattered not. She would teach her children all she knew of her trade, from using lime to tan fresh skins into leather right up to painting the finer details on a pair of court shoes. If they chose a different path…at least they would have an honest trade to fall back on, should they fail.

Alba became aware of Dalia's expectant eyes on her, as though she wanted an answer. "I'm sorry?" Alba said.

"Master Brogan wants to know how I saw through the false testimony your brothers concocted for the man who runs the salt mine. My answer was silk. I have seen you in sacking and wool and linen, but never anything else. How often have you worn silk?"

If this was a trick or a test, Alba didn't know what the woman wanted to hear. So she told the truth: "Never. When Brogan had clothes made for me that might break the curse, there was a lovely dress of fine silk, the sort I imagine courtiers wear with the shoes I make. But such things are not for women who work, like I do, so I chose to wear the wool instead, and that only with an apron to cover it. I'd ruin it with paint splatters before the day was through. A terrible waste of something so fine."

Dalia inclined her head. "A fine sentiment, but there will be an occasion soon where you will have little time for work. Your wedding day, I believe. You should wear the silk dress then."

And with that, she left.

Sixty-One

They were wed not in the grand cathedral, but in a small wooden church near where Brogan had grown up. His family and friends filled the place, leaving Alba no room to regret that she had no family or close friends to invite. She'd lost all her childhood friends when her brothers had taken her from the city, and it would take time to reacquaint herself with her neighbours.

As Dalia had suggested, Alba wore the azure silk gown Brogan had bought her to break the curse, topped with the ultramarine cloak.

Though both should have been too small, the witch had worked her magic over all the clothes Brogan had bought for her, including the boots he'd made. He'd slid them onto her feet himself that very morning, and she had to admit she could scarcely wait until the time came for him to help her out of both the boots and her gown.

But in the meantime, she was too busy meeting and greeting their guests, accepting their congratulations and trying to remember all the new names. No one seemed to mind her frequent blushes, when her thoughts strayed to last night in the loft, or the wedding night to come.

Brogan's new niece squalled loudly, though Alba wagered she'd scream even louder at her baptism the following week, when the priest doused her in cold water. She doubted even her gift of christening shoes would quiet the child.

Would her son be more like her, or Brogan? Alba's hand flew to her belly, though it was still too early for her pregnancy to show. She was only a few days late – if Dalia hadn't already told her about the baby, she would not yet have suspected his existence. But she'd seen the knowing glances that passed between the guests, whenever anyone mentioned how quickly she and Brogan had chosen to wed.

Let them think what they wished. She had married the man she loved, and together, they were building a future they could one day share with their son, and all their other children.

And if she ever told the tale of the elves and the shoemaker to her children, it would be about how the shoemaker and his wife freed the elves, who ran away with their new clothes, never to be seen again. A pretty story that would not feed childish nightmares, like the truth would do.

"Where is the Master Shoemaker?"

The crowd parted to allow a guard through. Not a city guard – he wore the tabard of the palace guard, not something often seen in this part of town.

"I am Master Brogan." Brogan's fingers slipped out of her grasp as he stepped forward to meet the guard.

"You must come with me, Master Brogan,"

the guard said.

"But it's his wedding day!" Brogan's brother, Gereon, shouted. "He hasn't yet bedded his bride!"

Titters erupted from the guests.

But not from the expressionless guard. "The Master Shoemaker and his wife are commanded to come to the palace for a royal audience."

Dalia had a hand in this, Alba was certain. For who else knew Brogan was to be married here today, aside from the assembled guests?

A dozen hands helped Alba smooth her hair and set her clothes straight, while others did the same for Brogan. When they were pronounced good enough to go to court, the crowd parted to let them and the guard leave.

To Alba's surprise, a carriage waited for them, adorned with the white eagle crest of the King. The guard sat in front with the driver, leaving her alone with Brogan.

He laced his fingers through hers. "Do you think the King will mind if I kiss you in his carriage?"

"He will never know," she replied, before

his lips touched hers.

Several kisses later, the carriage slowed as it entered the castle walls. Reluctantly, they broke apart.

Servants opened the carriage door and offered Alba assistance in stepping down. The palace guard had gone, and a well-dressed woman approached, then curtseyed. "Follow me," she said before Alba could do the same.

Brogan's hand gripped hers as the noblewoman led the way into the castle. Not to the public halls, but higher, to the private chambers where the royal family lived.

"Your Majesty, the Master Shoemaker," the woman said, before curtseying so low her skirt puddled around her.

The woman rose and moved aside, gesturing for them to enter.

The girl who had made the Crown Princess's christening shoes would have hung back, fearful of what awaited her.

But Alba was no longer that frightened girl. She stepped across the threshold first, bringing Brogan with her through the strength of their joined hands.

Three steps into the small chamber, she had to stop or crash into the room's sole occupant, a woman who wasn't much older than she was, though her heavily pregnant belly said she had been married longer.

Mindful of her manners, Alba curtseyed, too, her silk skirts spreading out in a shimmering pool. A glimpse of red made her raise her head just a little until her gaze fixed on the Queen's boots. Whoever had coloured the leather had spread a thin tint of vermillion over an already warm brown, instead of bleaching the leather and using the proper amount of vermillion to create the rich red royalty deserved.

"Master Shoemaker, I have summoned you to have some shoes made for my daughter's betrothal to the Viken prince," the Queen said.

"What does Your Majesty have in mind?" Brogan asked.

"Half my court wears shoes made from your shop. Even some of my ladies. Each with designs as different as the women who wear them, never the same. They say your power to produce perfection borders on the miraculous.

Exactly what I want in my Royal Shoemaker. What sort of shoes would you make, on the occasion where two kingdoms are to be joined?"

"Vermillion slippers, bright as fresh blood, adorned with a white eagle, its wings spread for flight across the front," Alba blurted out, spreading her fingers across the Queen's shoe to demonstrate. "Perhaps a gold crown on the heel, if you wish for more height, but if it is a state occasion, surely you will wear a dress with a train, so no one will see the heels. What colour will your gown be?"

Alba raised her head to find both the Queen and her husband staring at her.

"Ah…Your Majesty," she added.

"Does your wife often speak for you, Master Shoemaker?" the Queen asked.

Brogan coughed, though it sounded more like a laugh he was trying to hide. "Your Majesty, I may be a Master Shoemaker, but my wife's work is what graces your court, not mine. She was the Royal Shoemaker when I was little more than an apprentice. That she chose me to work alongside her in her late father's, the former Royal Shoemaker's, shop, is an honour I fear I do not deserve."

"No one told me the Royal Shoemaker was a woman," the Queen said.

Alba felt her cheeks redden. "My father was the last official Royal Shoemaker, Your Majesty. Though during the illness that took his life, I made most of the shoes that left our shop. The Crown Princess's christening shoes, for instance."

"They were exquisite. Her new sister will wear them at her christening." The Queen patted her belly for a moment, then turned her gaze on Alba once more. "Eagles and crowns, you say? Like my husband's family crest?"

"Like a mother eagle about to take flight to defend her nest, her amber eye fixed upon those who might threaten her and hers," Alba said, already envisioning the painting in her mind's eye. "Against a background of red, the colour of the blood she would shed to protect her kingdom and its allies."

The Queen leaned forward. "What colour gown would match such magnificent shoes?"

Alba thought for a moment. "White, with

red and gold embroidery. Perhaps a red veil over your hair, held in place with amber or gold. Forgo a train, if you wish your shoes to be seen properly, though I would suggest gilded crowns for the heels, which will glitter when they catch the light."

The Queen clapped her hands. "Oh, I like it! What is your name, Royal Shoemaker?"

When she realised Brogan had no intention of answering, for the question had definitely been directed at her, she replied, "Alba."

"Well, Alba, you may take my measurements now, so that you may start work," the Queen said, extending her foot. "As my Royal Shoemaker, I expect my shoes to take priority over any lesser commissions."

"Yes, Your Majesty," Alba said. "Would you like a pair of new boots to replace the ones you are wearing, too? I made some in a particularly soft black leather for the Crown Princess's godmother, Mistress Dalia the Enchantress. But for you, perhaps red or white…"

"Why not both?" the Queen interrupted eagerly.

"Why not indeed?"

By the time the Queen had finished ordering a dozen pairs of new shoes, dark evening clouds had replaced the sunny daytime skies, and the Queen sent them home in her carriage, complete with a substantial bag of gold to cover her purchases.

The carriage rolled to a stop, and the driver opened the door. Snow swirled in, as the last winter blizzard began to make its presence known.

Brogan bounded down to the cobblestones and held out his arms. "Mistress Royal Shoemaker, allow me to assist you."

He lifted her from the carriage, not letting her feet touch the ground until they were under his roof. A merry fire blazed in the hearth, and someone had laid out a veritable feast on the worktable. A barrel of mead sat at the foot of the ladder to the loft, with two cups waiting to be filled.

"I'll move some of this, so that we can start work right away on the Queen's commission," Brogan said, regret colouring his tone.

Alba held up her hand. "The Queen can

wait until tomorrow. Tonight, we are newly wed, and I have heard the most elaborate stories about what happens to a bride on her wedding night. We have the rest of our lives to work. Tonight, there shall be no shoes. Just you, and me, and maybe a jug of that mead, up in the loft."

"So no more working nights?" Brogan asked hopefully.

Alba closed her eyes. "Now the curse is broken, I am free. I shall be the Royal Shoemaker while the sun is in the sky, and once it sets, I will be your wife, and nothing else."

Brogan made a show of peering out the window. The wind slammed the shutter closed, so he bolted it. "It's too dark outside to see any sign of the sun, so come, wife, and let me show you what my bride deserves on her wedding night."

He held out his hands, then grasped her around the waist and lifted her up to the loft. He scrambled up after her.

Off came the silk gown, and the shift beneath, mixed with the wedding finery

Brogan shed as fast as his hands could unlace it.

When they were naked, she grabbed him, tumbling him into bed. Beneath the blankets, they made love as husband and wife for the first time, and the second, and, much later, a third, for they agreed that newlyweds can never have too much practice at such things.

The storm raged outside, but Alba and Brogan noticed none of it, for they had finally found and united the perfect pair.

About the Author

Demelza Carlton has always loved the ocean, but on her first snorkelling trip she found she was afraid of fish.

She has since swum with sea lions, sharks and sea cucumbers and stood on spray drenched cliffs over a seething sea as a seven-metre cyclonic swell surged in, shattering a shipwreck below.

Demelza now lives in Perth, Western Australia, the shark attack capital of the world.

The *Ocean's Gift* series was her first foray into fiction, followed by her suspense thriller *Nightmares* trilogy. She swears the *Mel Goes to Hell* series ambushed her on a crowded train and wouldn't leave her alone.

Want to know more? You can follow Demelza on Facebook, Twitter, YouTube or her website, Demelza Carlton's Place at:

www.demelzacarlton.com

Books by Demelza Carlton

Siren of Secrets series

Ocean's Secret (#1)
Ocean's Gift (#2)
Ocean's Infiltrator (#3

Siren of War series

Ocean's Justice (#1)
Ocean's Widow (#2)
Ocean's Bride (#3)
Ocean's Rise (#4)
Ocean's War (#5)
How To Catch Crabs

Nightmares Trilogy

Nightmares of Caitlin Lockyer (#1)
Necessary Evil of Nathan Miller (#2)
Afterlife of Alana Miller (#3)

Mel Goes to Hell series

The Devil's Work (#1)
See You in Hell (#2)
Mel Goes to Hell (#3)
To Hell and Back (#4)
The Holiday From Hell (#5)
All Hell Breaks Loose (#6)
The Devil Goes to Heaven (#7)

Romance Island Resort series

Maid for the Rock Star (#1)
The Rock Star's Email Order Bride (#2)
The Rock Star's Virginity (#3)
The Rock Star and the Billionaire (#4)
The Rock Star Wants A Wife (#5)
The Rock Star's Wedding (#6)
Maid for the South Pole (#7)

Romance a Medieval Fairytale series

Enchant: Beauty and the Beast Retold
Dance: Cinderella Retold
Fly: Goose Girl Retold
Revel: Twelve Dancing Princesses Retold
Silence: Little Mermaid Retold
Awaken: Sleeping Beauty Retold
Embellish: Brave Little Tailor Retold
Appease: Princess and the Pea Retold
Blow: Three Little Pigs Retold
Return: Hansel and Gretel Retold
Wish: Aladdin Retold
Melt: Snow Queen Retold
Spin: Rumpelstiltskin Retold
Kiss: Frog Prince Retold
Reflect: Snow White Retold
Roar: Goldilocks Retold
Cobble: Elves and the Shoemaker Retold
Float: Enchanted Horse Retold
Steal: Forty Thieves Retold
Call: Pied Piper Retold